—

The Christmas Swap

A holiday they won't forget!

Nurse Luci Dawson and Dr Cal Hollingsworth have both had their lives turned upside down. So when they get the chance to swap houses in the run-up to Christmas it could be just what they need to start afresh for the festive season!

Find out what happens in:

Waking Up to Dr Gorgeous
by Emily Forbes

and

Swept Away by the Seductive Stranger
by Amy Andrews

Available now!

Dear Reader,

I wrote my first ten books with my sister, and in my experience the first thing everyone asked was, 'How do you do it?' The truth was I'd never written a book any other way—that was all I knew. I have now written fifteen stories solo, but when I was asked if I would be interested in writing a duo with Amy Andrews of course I said yes. We have known each other for a long time, and Amy has also written books with her sister, so we're both used to plotting with other writers—and sometimes negotiating! ☺

Working out our characters and our stories and how we were going to fit them together was great fun. Our brief was simply to write two stories in which our characters swapped houses; the rest was up to us. We took one character from the country and sent her to the city, and moved one hero in the other direction. One country girl, one city boy—both out of their depth.

Seb and Callum Hollingsworth are gorgeous, smart, sexy brothers, and Luci and Flick are best friends. Even though it might have made sense to make the girls sisters, as that's what we both know so well, it was more interesting to make the boys siblings—two brooding loners in need of a bit of loving.

I really hope you enjoy both stories.

Happy reading,

Emily

WAKING UP TO DR GORGEOUS

BY
EMILY FORBES

HarperCollins
PUBLISHERS
Since 1817

First published in Great Britain 2016
By Mills & Boon, an imprint of HarperCollins*Publishers*
1 London Bridge Street, London, SE1 9GF

Large Print edition 2017

© 2016 Emily Forbes

ISBN: 978-0-263-06689-0

Our policy is to use papers that are natural, renewable
and recyclable products and made from wood grown
in sustainable forests. The logging and manufacturing
processes conform to the legal environmental
regulations of the country of origin.

Printed and bound in Great Britain
by CPI Antony Rowe, Chippenham, Wiltshire

Emily Forbes is an award-winning author of Medical Romances for Mills & Boon. She has written over 25 books and has twice been a finalist in the Australian Romantic Book of the Year Award, which she won in 2013 for her novel *Sydney Harbour Hospital: Bella's Wishlist*. You can get in touch with Emily at emilyforbes@internode.on.net, or visit her website at emily-forbesauthor.com.

Books by Emily Forbes

Mills & Boon Medical Romance

The Hollywood Hills Clinic

Falling for the Single Dad

Tempted & Tamed!

A Doctor by Day...
Tamed by the Renegade

Sydney Harbour Hospital: Bella's Wishlist
Breaking the Playboy's Rules
Daring to Date Dr Celebrity
The Honourable Army Doc
A Kiss to Melt Her Heart
His Little Christmas Miracle
A Love Against All Odds

Visit the Author Profile page at millsandboon.co.uk for more titles.

For anyone who has ever fallen in love
when they didn't intend to—
it's never the wrong time!

**Praise for
Emily Forbes**

'*The Honourable Army Doc* was a
wonderful, emotional and passionate read
that I recommend to all readers.'

—Goodreads

'Have your tissues ready because you
are gonna need them…it's that good!
Prepare to be hooked on Medical Romance
and Emily Forbes!'

—Goodreads on
A Love Against All Odds

CHAPTER ONE

'OMG, FLICK, I wish you'd been able to see this place.'

Luci had spoken to her best friend several times already today but she couldn't resist calling her again to update her on her good fortune.

'It's nice, then?' She could hear the smile in Flick's voice.

'Nice! It's amazing.' Luci wandered around the apartment while she chatted. 'It's right on the harbour. The beach is just across the road. I'm looking at the sea as we speak.' She could hear the waves washing onto the shore and smell the salt in the air. 'I don't know how Callum is going to manage in my little house.'

It was a bit odd to be walking around a stranger's apartment. Luci had spent her whole life surrounded by people she knew so to travel halfway across the country to swap houses with a stranger was odd on so many levels. It had all happened so quickly she hadn't had time to consider how it would feel. Callum Hollingsworth's apartment on the shores of Sydney Harbour was modern and masculine. While her house wasn't particularly feminine it was old and decorated in what she guessed people would call country style. No surprises there, it was definitely a country house. It was clear that her house-swap partner's taste in decorating was quite different from hers. She felt self-conscious, wondering what he would think of her place, before she realised it didn't matter. She didn't plan on meeting the guy.

She heard the whistle of the Indian Pacific through the phone. The two friends had spent the past few days chilling on Bondi Beach, a girls' getaway that Flick had suggested before Luci settled into her house swap and study course in Sydney, and Flick returned to South Australia on the iconic trans-continental train.

'Are you on the train?' Luci asked.

'Not yet,' Flick replied. 'I'm just grabbing a coffee and waiting to board.'

'Make sure you call me when you get home,' she told her.

'Of course I will. What are you going to do with the rest of your day?'

'I think I'll take a stroll around my new neighbourhood. The hospital is a half-hour walk away so I might head in that direction. Work out where I have to be tomorrow. I don't want to be late.' Luci was enrolled in an eight-week course in child and family health being run through the North Sydney Hospital and she needed to get her bearings. 'Look after my mum and dad for me.'

That was her one big concern. As an only child of elderly parents—her mother called her their 'change of life' baby—Luci was nervous about being so far away from them, but Flick had promised to keep an eye on them. It wasn't hard for her to do as Luci's dad was the local doctor and Flick worked for him as a practice nurse.

'I will. Enjoy yourself.'

Luci ended the call and had another wander

around. It wasn't a massive apartment—there was an open-plan kitchen, living and dining room with a large balcony that looked out to the beach across the road. Two bedrooms, two bathrooms and a small laundry finished it off, but it had everything she would need. She dumped her bags in the spare bedroom. Having the two bedrooms was a bonus because she didn't feel comfortable about taking over Callum's room. That felt too familiar.

The sun shone on the water of Sydney Harbour, white boats bobbed and the houses peeked out between eucalyptus trees. Luci couldn't believe how perfect it looked. She'd grown up in country South Australia, born and bred in Vickers Hill in the Clare Valley, and she'd never travelled far. Her father very rarely took holidays and when he did they spent them on the coast, but the coast she was familiar with was the Gulf of St Vincent with its calm waters, like a mill pond. It never felt like the real ocean.

Then, when she'd married her high-school sweetheart at the age of twenty-one, they'd had no money for holidays. She'd married young, as had most of her friends, but she hadn't found the happy-ever-after she'd wanted. Like so many other marriages, hers hadn't lasted and she found herself divorced and heartbroken at twenty-five.

But now, perhaps, it was time to travel. To see something of the world. She couldn't change what had happened, the past was the past. She had grieved for a year, grieved for the things she had lost—her marriage, her best friend and her dream of motherhood—but she was recovering now and she refused to believe that her life was over. Far from it. She had a chance now to reinvent herself. Her teenage dream needed some remodelling and this was her opportunity to figure out a new direction, if that's what she decided she wanted. She was finally appreciating the freedom she had been given; she was no longer defined by her status as daughter, girlfriend or wife. No one in Sydney knew anything about her. She was just Luci.

It was time to start again.

* * *

Luci turned off the shower and wrapped herself in one of the fluffy towels that she'd found in the guest bathroom. She pulled the elastic band from her hair, undoing the messy bun that had kept her shoulder-length bobbed blonde hair dry, then dried herself off. She was exhausted and she was looking forward to climbing into bed. She was far more tired than she'd expected to be. She'd spent the past three days sitting in lectures. She'd thought that would be easier than the shift work on the wards that she was used to, but it was mentally tiring.

Still, it was almost the end of her first week. Only two more days to go before the weekend. Perhaps then she'd have a chance to see something of this side of Sydney. She and Flick had walked from Bondi to Bronte and back and had spent the rest of their time relaxing. Sightseeing hadn't been high on their agenda but Luci had never visited Sydney before and she wanted to get a feel for the city.

She was familiar with the route from Callum's

apartment in Fairlight to the hospital on the opposite side of the Manly peninsula as she was walking that route every day. She was getting to know the local shopkeepers and was exchanging 'good mornings' with a couple of regular dog walkers. It was a far cry from Vickers Hill, where she couldn't take two steps down the main street without bumping into someone she knew, but she was starting to feel a little more at home here. She kept herself busy, not wanting to give herself a chance to be homesick. Being somewhere new was exciting, she told herself, and she had limited time so she needed to make the most of her opportunities.

The people in her course were getting friendlier by the day. It seemed city folk took a little longer to warm up to strangers but Luci had gone out to dinner tonight with a few of them, just a burger in Manly, but it was a start and Luci knew she'd feel even more at home after another week.

She knew where to catch the ferry to the city and she'd walked on the beach but she hadn't yet had time to test the water in the tidal swimming pool that was built into the rocks. That would be added to her list of things to do. She hadn't done nearly as much exploring as she had planned to, and if all the weeks were this busy, her two months in Sydney would fly past. She'd have to make time to see the sights, but first she needed some sleep.

She hung the towel on the rail in the bathroom, went through to her bedroom and slid naked between her bedsheets. She kept the window blinds up and the window slightly open. From the bed she could see the stars in the sky and the sound of the ocean carried to her on the warm spring air. The ocean murmured to itself as it lapped the shore. It was gentle tonight and she could imagine the waves kissing the sand, teasing gently before retreating, only to come back for more.

She dozed off to the sound of the sea.

It felt like only moments later that she woke to an unfamiliar sound. A slamming door.

She was still getting used to the different sounds and rhythms of the city. She could sleep through the early morning crowing of a rooster and the deep rumble of a tractor but the slightest noise in the middle of suburbia disturbed her. Rubbish trucks, the tooting of ferry horns, slamming of car doors and the loud conversations of late-night commuters or drinking buddies on their way home from the pub all intruded on her dreams, but this noise was louder than all of those. This noise was close.

She heard footsteps on the wooden floorboards and saw light streaming under her bedroom door as the passage light flicked on.

Shit. There was someone in the house.

She put her hand on her chest. Her heart was racing.

What should she do?

Call out?

No, that would only draw attention to herself.

Find a weapon of some sort? She'd seen a set of golf clubs but they were in a cupboard near the front door. She couldn't get to them and there was nothing in the bedroom. Maybe a shot of hair spray to the face would work—if only she used hairspray.

Should she call the police? But how quickly would they get here? Not fast enough, she assumed.

She had no idea what to do. She'd never had to fend for herself.

She sat up in bed, and scrabbled for her phone in the dark. She was too afraid to turn on the light, worried it would draw the attention of the intruder. She clutched the sheet to her chest to cover her nakedness. Perhaps she should find some clothes first. She didn't want to confront a burglar while naked.

She could hear him crossing the living room. The tread of the steps were heavy. Man heavy. She could hear boots. The steps weren't light and delicate. He wasn't making any attempt to be quiet. There was a loud thump as something soft but weighty hit the floor. It didn't sound like a person. A bag maybe? A bag of stolen goods?

Her heart was still racing and the frantic pounding almost drowned out the sound of the footsteps. That made her pause. This had to be the world's noisiest burglar. She hadn't had much experience with burglars but surely they would generally try to be quiet? This one was making absolutely no attempt to be silent. Plus he had turned the lights on. Definitely not stealthy.

He was a terrible burglar, possibly one of the worst ever.

But maybe he thought the house was empty? Perhaps she should make some noise? Enough noise for two people.

She heard the soft pop as the seal on the fridge door was broken. She frowned. Now he was looking in the fridge? Making himself at home. She was positive it wasn't Callum. Luci had spoken to Flick earlier in the day. Callum had well and truly arrived in Vickers Hill and according to her friend he was creating a bit of a stir. Luci hoped he wasn't going to prove difficult—he was supposed to be making things easier for her dad, not harder, but she couldn't do much about it. All it meant to her was that it wasn't Callum in the apartment. And she was pretty sure by now that it wasn't a burglar either, but that still meant a stranger was in the house.

She needed to get dressed.

She switched on the bedside light and was halfway out of bed when she heard the footsteps moving along the passage. While she was debating her options she saw the bedroom door handle moving.

OMG, they were coming in.

'You'd better get out of here. I've called the police,' she yelled, not knowing what else to do.

The door handle continued to turn and a voice said, 'You've done what?'

When it became obvious that the person who belonged to the voice was intent on entering her room she jumped back into bed and pulled the covers up to her chin, grabbing her phone just in case she did need to call the cops.

'I'll scream,' she added for good measure.

But the door continued to open and a vision appeared. Luci wondered briefly if she was dreaming. Her heart was racing at a million miles an hour but now she had no clue whether it was due to nerves, fear, panic or simple lust. This intruder might just be the most gorgeous man she'd ever laid eyes on. Surely someone this gorgeous couldn't be evil?

But then Ted Bundy sprang to mind. He was a good-looking, charming, educated man who just happened to be a serial killer. 'Don't come any closer,' she said.

He stopped and held his hands out to his sides. 'I'm not going to hurt you, but who the hell are you and what are you doing in my room?' he said.

'*Your* room?'

Was this Callum? She was certain she'd chosen the guest bedroom but, anyway, what was he doing here? He couldn't have got back to Sydney that quickly. He was supposed to be a thousand miles away, staying in her house. That was how a house swap worked. 'Why aren't you in Vickers Hill?'

'What the heck is Vickers Hill?'

Luci frowned. 'Who are you?'

He couldn't be Callum. So whose room was she in exactly?

'Seb. Seb Hollingsworth.'

Seb.

'You're not Callum?'

A crease appeared between his superb blue eyes as he frowned. 'No. I'm his brother.'

Luci almost missed his answer, distracted as she was by the thick, dark eyelashes that framed his eyes.

'Brother!' Why hadn't Callum warned her? She sat up in the bed, taking care to make sure the sheets prevented any sort of indecent exposure. 'Callum didn't mention you.'

'So you do know Cal, then?'

'Sort of.'

He lifted one eyebrow but said nothing.

Luci could play that game too. And she used the silent seconds to examine the vision a little more closely.

He truly was gorgeous. Tall, really tall, with thick dark hair, chestnut she'd call it. He had eyebrows to match that shaded piercing blue eyes and a nose that may or may not have been broken once upon a time. His lips were full and pink, and a two-day growth of beard darkened his jaw.

His torso was bare but he held what appeared to be a black T-shirt in his hand. Just what had he been planning on doing? she wondered, before she was distracted again by his broad shoulders and smooth chest. He reminded her of someone, she thought as her eyes roamed over his body.

The statue of David, she thought, brought to life. He was made of warm flesh instead of cool marble but had the same, startling level of perfection.

Her heart was still beating a rapid tattoo. Adrenaline was still coursing through her system but not out of fear. Now it was a simple chemical, or maybe hormonal, reaction.

'I think you have some explaining to do,' said the living, breathing statue.

In Luci's opinion so did Callum, Seb's absent brother, and she was blowed if she was going to explain herself while she lay in bed naked. She clutched the sheet a little more tightly across her breasts. 'Let me get dressed and then we can talk.'

The corner of Seb's mouth lifted in a wry smile and there was a wicked gleam in his blue eyes. Luci felt a burst of heat explode in her belly and she knew that the heat would taint her body with a blush of pink. She could feel the warmth spreading up over her chest and neck as Seb continued to stand in the doorway. Did he know the effect he was having on her? She had to get rid of him.

'Can you give me a minute?' she asked.

'Sure, sorry,' he replied, looking anything but sorry. 'And while you're at it,' he added, glancing at the phone that was still clutched in her hand along with the sheet, 'do you think you could ring the police and tell them it was just a misunderstanding? I don't want the neighbours getting the wrong idea.'

'I didn't actually ring the police,' Luci admitted.

He turned and left the room, pulling the door closed behind him, and she could hear him laughing, a deep, cheerful sound that lifted her spirits.

Luci waited to hear his footsteps retreat before she was brave enough to throw off the sheets once more. She climbed out of bed on shaky legs and pulled on a T-shirt and a pair of shorts. She padded down the hallway to the open-plan lounge and kitchen to find Seb with his head in the fridge, giving her a very nice view of a tidy rear covered in denim. His bare feet poked out of the bottom of his jeans.

She stepped around a pile of luggage that had been dumped beside the couch. A brown leather jacket was draped over a duffel bag and a motor-bike helmet sat on the floor beside a pair of sturdy boots, the boots that had been stomping down the passage. There was a thick layer of reddish-brown dust covering everything.

She ducked through the kitchen and into the dining area, where she stood on the far side of the table, putting some distance between them. Despite the fact that he looked like something created by Michelangelo and appeared to be re-lated to the owner of the house, she wasn't pre-pared to take his word for it just yet. Until she'd decided he wasn't a serial killer she wasn't taking any chances.

He stood up and turned to face her. His chest was now covered by his black T-shirt—that was a pity—and he had two small bottles of beer in his hand.

'Beer?' he asked as he raised his hand.

Luci shook her head.

He put one bottle back in the fridge, closed the door and then twisted the top off the other bottle and took a swig. He watched her as she watched him but he didn't seem as nervous as her. Not nearly.

He stepped over to the table, pulled out a chair and sat down. He pushed the chair back and stretched his legs out. He was tall. His legs were long. He was fiddling with the beer bottle and she couldn't help but notice that his fingers were long and slender too.

He lifted his eyes up to meet her gaze. 'So, sleeping beauty, do you have a name?'

'Luci.'

'Luci,' he repeated, stretching out the two syllables, and the way the 'u' rolled off his tongue did funny things to her insides.

'So where's my big brother? And why are you in my bed?'

Luci swallowed nervously. His bed? Of course, his room, his bed. That warmth in her belly spread lower now, threatening to melt her already wobbly legs just a little bit more.

'I didn't know it was your bed. I didn't know anyone else lived here.'

Callum hadn't said anything but she'd never actually spoken to Callum. Not that she was about to divulge that bit of information. That would just come across as odd. Her dad's practice manager had organised the whole house-swap thing. Luci had exchanged emails with Callum and had been intending on meeting to swap keys but he had messaged her to say his plans had changed. He'd left Sydney a day earlier than they had discussed so he'd left a key under a flowerpot for her, but she was certain he hadn't mentioned a brother. Not at any stage.

So what did this mean for her house-sitting plans? Would Seb ask her to leave? Would Callum?

'So where is he?' Seb wanted to know. 'Should I be checking the rest of the house? You haven't done away with him, have you? Did he treat you badly and you've sneaked in here to have your revenge?'

Luci laughed and wondered about the type of women Seb associated with if that was the direction his thoughts took him. 'He's in Vickers Hill.'

'Ah, Vickers Hill. You mentioned it before. Where is that exactly?' Seb arched his right eyebrow again and Luci found herself wondering if he could also do that with the left one. The idea distracted her and she almost forgot his question.

'In South Australia. In the Clare Valley,' she explained as she stepped into the kitchen. She needed to put some distance between them. To give herself something to do, she switched the kettle on, taking a mug and a green tea bag from the cupboard.

Seb took another pull of his beer. 'What is he doing there?'

'He's gone to work in a general practice. It's part of his studies.' She didn't mention that he was working with her father. If Callum wanted his brother to know what he was up to, he could tell him the finer details. But Seb not knowing Callum's movements only led to more questions. Where had Seb been? Why didn't he know what was happening? His room certainly didn't look inhabited. It had looked exactly like a guest room, which was what Luci had expected. There had been no sign of his presence other than a few clothes in the wardrobe, which she had assumed was the overflow from Callum's room. But perhaps those clothes belonged to Seb.

'So, if Cal's in Vickers Hill, what are you doing here?'

'We've done a house swap,' she replied as she poured boiled water into her mug.

'A house swap?' he repeated. 'How long are you staying?'

'Eight weeks. Until Christmas.' *Please, don't ask me to leave tonight*, she thought. She was half-resigned to the fact that her plans were about to change but she really didn't want to pack her bags and find somewhere else to stay in the middle of the night. This was her first trip to Sydney. 'If that's all right,' she added, pleading desperately. She had no idea where she'd go if he asked her to leave. Back to Bondi, she supposed, but the prospect of doing that at this late hour was not at all appealing.

Seb shrugged. 'It's Cal's house, whatever plans you've made with him stick. I just crash here when I'm in town. I called it my room but, I guess, technically it's not.'

Luci wondered where he'd been. Where he'd come from. But she was too tired to think about that now.

'I'll stay in Callum's room,' he added.

'Thank you.' She threw her tea bag in the bin and picked up her mug. 'I guess I'll see you in the morning, then.'

She took her tea and retreated. Seb looked interesting and she was certainly intrigued. He was giving her more questions than answers and she needed, wanted, to find out more, but it would have to wait. She had to get some sleep.

But sleep eluded her. She tossed and turned and wondered about Seb. Maybe she should have just stayed up and got all the answers tonight. Instead she lay in bed and made up stories in her head, filling in all the blank spaces about the handsome stranger with imagined details.

It wasn't often she got to meet a stranger. And a gorgeous, fascinating one to boot. In Vickers Hill everyone knew everyone else and their business. Meeting someone new was quite thrilling compared to what she was used to. Excitement bubbled in her chest. A whole new world of possibilities might open up to her.

She smiled to herself as she rolled over.

Things had just become interesting.

CHAPTER TWO

SEB PUT HIS empty beer bottle down on the kitchen table and stared out at the dark ocean through the branches of the eucalyptus. He could hear the waves lapping on the shore and could see the lights of the yachts rising and falling on the water. He'd missed the sound of the ocean but he wasn't thinking about the water or the boats or the lights now. He was thinking about the woman he'd found in his bed. The absolutely stunning, and very naked, woman.

It had been a surprise, to put it mildly. He detested surprises normally—experience had taught him that they were generally unpleasant—but he couldn't complain about this one. He'd found women in his bed unexpectedly before but he couldn't recall any of them being quite as attractive as Luci.

He closed his eyes but his mind was restless and he couldn't settle. He should be exhausted. He'd had a long and dusty eight-hour ride from Deniliquin and he'd been looking forward to a shower, something to eat and then bed. In that order. That had been his plan until he'd discovered Luci in his bed. His plan had been delightfully disrupted by a gorgeous naked woman.

He wasn't sure that he really understood why she was here. Or why Cal wasn't. He hadn't spoken to his brother for several weeks. They didn't have that sort of relationship. Seb wasn't even in the habit of calling ahead to let Callum know he would be in town. They were close but unless there was a reason for a call neither of them picked up the phone. And when they did their conversations were brief, borne out of necessity only and usually avoided if possible.

Seb had tried to talk to Cal after Cal had been injured in a cricketing accident, an accident that had almost cost him his left eye, but even then they had never got to the heart of the problem.

Neither of them were much good at discussing their feelings.

But despite their lack of communication they still shared a brotherly bond. They had relied on each other growing up. The sons of high-achieving surgeons, they had spent a lot of time by themselves, supervised only by nannies. Perhaps that was why they had never learned to discuss their feelings—the nannies certainly hadn't encouraged it and Seb couldn't remember many family dinners or even much support in times of crisis. Not that there had been many crises, just one big one for each of them in their adult lives. They'd been lucky really.

But their childhood bonds had remained strong and Cal had always had a bed for him. Until now. Which brought him back to the question of what Luci was really doing here. And what did it mean for him?

He ran his hands through his hair. It was thick with dust and sweat from hours encased in a helmet. He still needed a shower. The sea breeze wafted through the balcony doors, carrying with it the fresh scent of salt. Perhaps he should go for a swim instead. The cool water of Sydney Harbour might be just what he needed to stop his brain from turning in circles.

There was no light coming from under Luci's door so he stripped off his jeans in the living room and pulled a pair of swimming shorts from his duffel bag. He left his house key under the flowerpot on the back balcony and jogged barefooted down the stairs and crossed the road to the beach. The sand was cool and damp under his feet and the water was fresh.

He didn't hesitate. He took three steps into the sea and dived under the water. He surfaced several metres offshore but the water was shallow enough that he could still stand. The sea was calm and gentle and refreshing but it wasn't enough to stop his head from spinning with unanswered questions.

Vickers Hill, South Australia. He'd never heard of Vickers Hill. How the hell had Callum ever found it? But if the girls there looked like Luci, he couldn't blame him for wanting to visit.

He turned and looked back across the beach to the apartment block. It was a small complex, only three floors, and Callum's apartment took up the top floor, but there was nothing to see as it was all in darkness. But he could imagine Luci, sleeping in his bed. The image of her, at the moment he'd first seen her, filled his mind.

In his bed with the sheets pulled up to her chin, her blue-grey eyes huge with apprehension. He'd got just as much of a shock as she had but at least he'd been semi-clothed. He'd been unable to see anything but he'd known that beneath those sheets, his sheets, she had been as naked as the day she was born.

As she had sat up in bed the covers had slipped down, exposing the swell of her breasts, before she'd clutched the sheet tightly, pulling it firmly across her chest. He'd had his T-shirt in his hand, halfway to the shower when he'd discovered her, and he'd had to surreptitiously move his hand so the T-shirt had covered his groin and his reaction. It had been pure and primal. Lust, desire.

He knew he'd let his eyes linger on her for a

few seconds too long to be considered polite. Had she noticed?

Her eyes had watched him carefully. Her face was round with a heart-shaped chin and she had lips like a ripe peach. She was thin but not skinny and she had firm, round breasts that it was impossible not to notice. He'd seen them rise and fall under the sheet as she'd panicked. He could have happily watched her breathing all night.

His eyes had been drawn to four small, dark freckles that made a diamond shape against the pale skin on her chest. One sat about an inch below her collarbone, another on the swell of her right breast with a matching one on the left, and the fourth one, the one that formed the bottom of the diamond, was tucked into her cleavage. The pattern was stamped on his memory.

He should have given her some privacy, backed out of the room, but he'd been transfixed.

He closed his eyes now and floated on his back but he could still see Luci's pale skin decorated with the perfect diamond imprinted on the backs of his eyelids. It was late and he was physically exhausted but he knew there was no way he'd be able to sleep. Not yet.

He flipped onto his front and swam further into the harbour. In the pale starlight he could see the outline of his boat tied to its mooring. With long, fluid strokes he passed several other boats floating on the water as he swam out to his cabin cruiser.

His hands gripped the ladder at the stern and he pulled himself up onto the small ledge at the rear. He ran his hand over the smooth, sleek lines of the cabin as he made his way round to the large, flat bow. He stretched, resting his back against the windscreen. This boat was his sanctuary. He'd bought it almost three years ago as a project. It had good lines and plenty of potential and had been advertised as needing some TLC or a handyman's touch. He was no builder but he was good with his hands and he'd figured the learning curve would keep his mind occupied, which was just what he'd needed at the time. He had needed a project, a focus, something to keep him busy, so he could avoid dealing with his alternate reality.

Three years down the track he had made good progress emotionally but he couldn't say the same about the boat. It was still far from finished, although he had managed to get it to the stage where he could enjoy a day out. The engine worked, as did the toilet, but the kitchen and sleeping berths still needed serious attention. That was his current project, one he intended to finish while he was back in Sydney this time. He had an appointment scheduled for tomorrow evening to meet a cabinet-maker who was, hopefully, going to make new cupboards for the kitchen. While it was far from perfect, it didn't matter. It was perfect for him.

The boat represented freedom.

Seb didn't want to be tied down and the boat gave him a sense of having a place in the world without commitment. Eventually, when the renovation was completed, he planned to live aboard. Having a boat as his place of residence appealed immensely as he could close it up and leave or take it with him. It would be a fluid living arrangement, transient enough that he didn't have to think of living aboard as settling down. It wasn't a big commitment.

He wasn't ready for commitment. He'd tried it once, with disastrous results.

Luckily for him Callum didn't show any signs of settling down either, which meant he always had a place to crash. It was reassuring to know that he had a place to stay that didn't require any commitment from him. Was that immature behaviour? Perhaps. Irresponsible? Maybe. He hadn't thought about what he'd do if Callum ever did settle down. At least he hadn't until tonight.

Seeing someone else in his room—he always thought of it as his, even though he was an infrequent visitor—seeing Luci in his bed, made him wonder what he would do if Callum ever wanted to make changes. What if he wanted to rent out that room or live with a girlfriend? Either one would put *him* out on the street.

Was he being selfish? Taking advantage of Callum's generosity? Was it time he grew up and stopped relying on his big brother?

But no matter what Cal's intentions were, being tossed out onto the street by Luci was still a possibility if she was uncomfortable about having him share her space. He'd told her he would stick with Callum's plan but what if she decided she didn't want him there?

One thing at a time, he decided. He'd only been back for five minutes. It wasn't worth wasting time worrying about things that might not happen. It was far more enjoyable to spend his time thinking about a pretty blonde who was curled up in his bed.

Seb laced his fingers together and rested his hands behind his head as he looked up at the sky. There were no clouds, the sky was dark and clear, the stars bright against the inky blackness. He picked out the Southern Cross, its familiar diamond shape marking the sky reminding him of the other diamond he'd seen earlier.

Things were about to become interesting.

* * *

Luci was up early. She showered and grabbed a piece of fruit for breakfast, trying to keep the noise to a minimum. There was no sound from Seb's room and she didn't want to disturb him. She hadn't heard him come back in last night but his motorbike helmet, jacket and boots were still piled on the living room floor so she assumed he was sleeping. She stuffed her laptop into her bag and slung it across her body, biting into her apple as she walked out the front door.

Today was her last full day of lectures. Tomorrow she and the other nineteen registered and enrolled nurses would have orientation at whichever child and family health centre they had been assigned to for their placements, and the course would then become a mixture of theory and practice. Luci was looking forward to getting out of the lecture room and dipping her toe into the world of family and community health.

The lectures had been interesting but she wasn't used to sitting down all day. The training room was an internal one in the hospital. It was small and windowless and by the end of the day Luci was itching to get outside into the fresh air. She was planning on taking a walk along Manly beach to clear the cobwebs from her mind. She stretched her arms and back and rolled her shoulders as the group waited for the final lecturer of the day. The topic for the last session was indigenous health, which had the potential to be interesting, but Luci didn't envy the lecturer their four o'clock timeslot. She doubted she was the only one who was thinking ahead to the end of the day.

Luci heard the sound of the door click open and swing shut. It was followed by a murmur from the back of the room that intensified in volume as it swept down the stairs. The room had half a dozen rows of tiered seating and she was sitting near the front. The room was buzzing and Luci turned her head to see what had got everyone so excited.

Seb was at the end of her row, about to step down to the front of the room. What on earth was he doing here?

He shrugged out of his leather jacket and dropped his motorbike helmet on a chair. He was dressed casually in sand-coloured cotton trousers and a chambray blue shirt that brought out the colour of his eyes.

He looked seriously hot.

He pulled a USB stick from his shirt pocket and plugged it into the computer. *He was the lecturer?*

He looked up, ready to address the room, and his eyes scanned the group, running over the twenty or so attendees. Luci's stomach was churning with nerves and her palms were sweaty as she waited for him to pick her out in the room. It didn't take long.

He spotted her in the front row and smiled. His blue eyes were intensely bright in his ridiculously handsome face and Luci swore the entire room, including the two male nurses, caught their collective breath. Her knees wobbled and she was glad she was already sitting down.

'Hello.' He was looking straight at her and everything around her dissolved in a haze as she melted into his gaze. 'I am Dr Seb Hollings-worth.'

Dr! Did he just say Dr? The motorbike-riding, leather-jacketed, living, breathing marble statue was a doctor? Somehow he'd let that little piece of information slide.

Luci missed the rest of his introduction as she tried to remember if she'd told him what she did. She'd talked about the house swap but perhaps she hadn't told him she was a nurse, which might explain why he hadn't mentioned he was a doctor. It was hard to remember anything when he was standing right in front of her, looking at her a bit too often with his bright blue eyes.

His voice was strong and deep and confident and Luci could feel it roll through her like waves rolling onto the shore. His voice caressed her and she was tempted to close her eyes as she listened. Maybe then she would be able to concentrate.

He was talking confidently about the cultural differences between the indigenous communities and those families with European backgrounds and the impact that had on the health of the children.

'Indigenous families are often reluctant to bring their children to the health clinics because of the lessons history has taught them. Many are fearful but we know that early intervention and health checks save lives. Education is the key, not only by the health professionals but also by the schools. We know that educated people have a better standard of living and better health. We have been running playgroups and early learning sessions to encourage the families to come to the clinics and the hope is that the parents will then feel comfortable enough to enrol their kids in school. Our current focus from a health perspective is on nutrition and family support so for any of you who will spend time working with these communities during your placements you'll need to be aware of the cultural sensitivities.'

Luci knew she should be taking notes but she was too busy watching and listening. She hadn't been able to keep her eyes closed. It was too tempting to watch him. And she knew where to find him if she had any questions.

'Funding is an issue—nothing new there,' he was saying, 'but the health department will continue to lobby for that. Our stats show there are benefits with these early intervention health programmes.'

There were lots of questions as Seb tried to wrap up his session. Luci guessed they all wanted to prolong the time that he spent in the room and even when he dismissed the class several of them crowded around him like kids around the ice-cream truck.

Luci gathered her notebook and laptop and shoved them into her bag. She wasn't going to hang around. If he was finished by the time she was packed up she'd stop and talk to him, otherwise she'd leave. She picked up her bag and started up the steps.

'Luci! Can you wait a moment?' Seb's voice stopped her in her tracks.

She hesitated. She had nowhere she had to rush off to. She had no reason not to wait. She dumped her bag on a chair and sat down, aware that some of the other girls were looking at her curiously. That was okay. She was used to being stared at and talked about.

Seb finished his discussions with the other students and came over to her.

'*Dr* Hollingsworth?' Luci was determined to get the first words in but that didn't seem to faze Seb.

'Nurse Luci.' He was smiling at her, making her insides turn somersaults. Again. 'Have you got time for a drink?'

'Why?'

'It seems we have some things to discuss, I thought it might be nice to share our secrets over a drink.'

'I don't have any secrets,' she fibbed.

His grin widened. 'Everyone has secrets,' he said. He had his jacket and helmet tucked under one arm and he picked up Luci's bag with his other hand. 'Come on, I'll give you a lift.'

'Where are we going?'

Seb smirked, obviously sensing victory, and

replied, 'The Sandman, it's about halfway down the beach.'

The bar was on North Steyne Street, a little over a kilometre away. Luci had walked past it before. 'I'll meet you there,' she said. The walk would give her a chance to clear her head and hopefully time to get over her jitters. She wasn't sure if this was a good idea but she couldn't think of an excuse on the spot. She couldn't think of anything much when Seb looked at her and smiled.

Luci took her bag from Seb and slung it over her shoulder. When she reached the beach she rolled up the legs of her khaki pants and slid her canvas sneakers off her feet and walked along the sand. The late-afternoon sun bounced off the waves, turning the water silver. Kids with surfboards ran in and out of the ocean, their shouts drowning out the screeching of the seagulls. The beach was busy. She didn't know a soul but she was fine with that. Back home she couldn't walk down the street without bumping into half a dozen people she knew and it was a pleasant change to have anonymity, especially after the past six months. It wasn't always so great having everyone know your business.

She stepped off the beach opposite the bar. She walked on the grass to brush the sand from her feet then slipped her shoes back on. Seb had beaten her there and he lifted a hand in greeting as she crossed the street. As if she wouldn't have noticed him—the bar was busy but he was easily the most noticeable person there.

Somehow, despite the crowd, he'd managed to grab a table with a view of the beach. He stood up as she approached and offered her a stool, his motorbike helmet on a third stool, like a chaperone.

'What can I get you to drink?'

'What are you going to have?'

'A beer.'

'That sounds great, thank you.'

Sturdy Norfolk pines lined the foreshore, guarding the beach, and Luci watched the ocean through the frame of the trees. She took her phone out of her bag as Seb went to the bar and snapped a photo of the view. She sent it to Flick captioned,

After-work drinks, could get used to this! But she resisted saying anything about the company she was keeping. There was no way to describe how he made her feel. Nervous, excited, expectant. She was silly to feel those things, she knew nothing about him, and she knew she couldn't share her thoughts, Flick would think she'd gone crazy.

She slipped her phone into her bag as Seb came back to the table.

He handed her a glass. 'So, you're a nurse?'

'And you're a doctor.'

'I am. Is that how you met Callum? Through the hospital? How come I've never met you?'

Luci laughed. 'Which question do you want me to answer first?'

'Your choice.'

He was looking at her intently and her heart pounded in her chest. He made her feel nervous—a gorgeous man paying her attention. It was such an unfamiliar situation but she would have to admit she rather liked it. She didn't even mind the nerves. It was exciting.

She took a sip of her beer as she thought about which answer to give him.

'I've never actually met your brother. And I've never been to Sydney before, which would be why we've never met. Callum needed a place to stay and so did I. The house swap was convenient for both of us. Nothing more than that.'

Luci had been restless since her divorce and Flick had been pushing her to get out of Vickers Hill, but she'd needed more than a push. She was buying her ex's share of their house and she couldn't afford to pay her mortgage and rent elsewhere so it wasn't until the house-swap idea had been suggested that she'd been brave enough to actually put a plan in motion. Having the opportunity to study *and* have free accommodation had been a big deciding factor for her. Which brought her back to the matter at hand. Where was she going to be able to stay now? It would be extremely inconvenient if she had to change her plans.

'Callum didn't tell me that he had any other tenants,' she said. 'I suppose I could look into nurses' accommodation through the hospital if you want me to move out. Do you know if the hospital has any student accommodation? I'm afraid I don't know anyone in Sydney to stay with.'

Seb shook his head. 'You have more right to be there than I do. I told you, whatever plans you made with him stick. It's his place and I'm not even technically a tenant. I only crash there when I come to town. I can ask one of my mates to put me up.'

'When you come to town?' Luci queried. 'You're not employed at North Sydney?' She had assumed he was a staff doctor. 'Are you just a guest lecturer?'

'Not exactly.' Seb picked up his glass and Luci's eyes followed the path of his drink from the table to his lips. She watched as he took a long sip. She could scarcely believe she was sitting at a bar, having a drink with a stranger. She'd never been out with a man she'd just met. Not one on one. For as long as she could remember she had been part of a couple.

Seb made her feel nervous. But it was a good kind of nervous. An exciting kind.

He swallowed his beer and continued, 'I'm employed by the state health department and I'm based out of North Sydney Hospital but I spend most of my time in rural areas. There doesn't seem to be much point paying rent in the city, especially not at Sydney prices, for the few nights a month that I'm in town so I crash at Cal's.'

Disappointment washed over her. He was only in town a few nights a month. Did that mean he'd be gone again soon?

'If you're only here for a few days then I'm sure we can manage to share the space,' she suggested, hoping she sounded friendly and hospitable rather than desperate, but the truth was she'd quite like the company. While she was enjoying her anonymity she'd never lived on her own before—she'd left home and moved into university accommodation and then married Ben. She was finding Callum's apartment a bit too quiet. She liked the idea of having company and she had a feeling she could do a lot worse than Seb's.

'I need to be honest,' he replied. 'I'm here for longer than a few days this time, it'll be closer to six weeks, and in the interests of full disclosure I'll be working out of the community health centre attached to the hospital. Where will you be doing your placement?'

'There.' Because Luci was from interstate she'd been given the most convenient placement.

'So we'll be working together too,' Seb added, 'but if you're happy to share Cal's space for a few days, we could give it a trial and see how we go.' He smiled at her and Luci's heart flipped in her chest. 'If it doesn't work out, I'll find somewhere else to stay. How's that sound?'

It sounded all right to her but she paused while she pretended to give it some thought. She nodded. 'Okay.'

'That's settled, then.' He tapped his drink against hers. 'House mates it is.' He sipped his beer and asked, 'So tell me about Vickers Hill. Your family is there?'

Luci nodded. 'My parents. I work at the local hospital.'

'Is it a big town?'

'Big enough to need a hospital. Your typical country hospital. We have obstetrics and some aged-care beds and we do some minor surgery as well.'

'So why the change to family and community health?'

'I needed to get out.'

'Of the hospital?'

Luci shook her head. 'Of Vickers Hill.'

'Why?'

Luci sighed quietly. There was no point keeping everything a secret as she figured he'd find out most of it eventually anyway. His brother was in Vickers Hill, working with her father. There would be no secrets. Not that her father would talk about her but Luci knew there were patients who couldn't resist gossip. And if Callum looked anything like Seb did, Luci knew there'd be no shortage of patients booking appointments with the new doctor. 'I got divorced six months ago and I just felt I needed to get out of town for a while.'

'Has it been messy?'

'Not messy so much as awkward. My dad is the local doctor—Callum has gone to work in his clinic,' she explained, 'so everyone, and I mean everyone, knows me. My ex-husband and I grew up together, we dated since high school, got married at twenty-one and divorced at twenty-five.'

'You were together, what, ten years?'

'About that.'

'That's a long time. This must be tough for you.'

No one else, other than Flick and her parents, had really understood how her divorce had impacted on her but Seb had hit the nail on the head immediately.

Her divorce had turned her world upside down. Every day of her life had included Ben. He was part of her history. Their friendship and relationship had shaped her into the person she was today and it had been difficult to separate herself into her own person. Ben was wrapped up in her identity and she was having to shape a new one for herself. It had been tough. Really tough.

Perhaps it was the distance lending Seb perspective. Everyone at home seemed to be having just as much difficulty adjusting to Luci being single as she was, which was partly why she had decided, or agreed with Flick's suggestion, to leave. The locals weren't moving on as quickly as she would like, which had made things even more difficult for her. It had taken her a lot of adjusting but she was finally coming to terms with the end of her marriage, and she felt the process would be faster if she didn't have to contend with local opinion as well.

'It has been rough,' she admitted. 'I reckon a divorce is sad and stressful enough, without having an entire town involved. Because everyone knew us, had seen us grow up, they all seemed to think that our divorce was somehow their business. I was tired of everyone either feeling sorry for me because I couldn't keep my husband or offering to set me up with their nephew, grandson or best friend's boy.'

'So you ran away?'

He was watching her closely and Luci could

feel herself starting to blush. She wasn't used to such close attention. She turned away, breaking eye contact. 'It was time for a change.'

Feeling sorry for herself was self-indulgent. She needed to move on but in a town where everyone knew her business that was hard to do. The truth was she hadn't coped well at all but that was none of their business. That's why Flick had been able to talk her into this crazy idea to take a study break in Sydney, and looking around her now she had to admit that it hadn't been such a mad idea after all. She was actually feeling like she was able to put her marriage behind her. But the demise of her marriage had also cost her the chance of motherhood and that wasn't so easy to come to terms with.

But she preferred to think she was running towards her future rather than away from her past. She didn't want to get pigeonholed, which was the danger if she'd stayed put, but there was no need to explain everything. Seb didn't need to know it all. Unlike at home, she could choose to keep her secrets. This was her opportunity to tell people only what she wanted them to know and she intended to make the most of it.

'Well, I reckon there's plenty in Sydney to keep you so busy that you won't have time to think. And I promise not to introduce you to any eligible men. Unless you ask me to,' he added. He finished his beer, pushed back the cuff of his shirt and looked at his watch. 'I have a meeting to get to but can I give you a lift home first?' he asked as he picked up his helmet.

'That would be great,' she said, but she should have said no.

Seb offered her his leather jacket to wear for protection, just in case something untoward happened. His hands brushed hers as he slid the jacket over her arms and when his fingers brushed her neck as he fastened the strap of his spare helmet under her chin Luci thought she might melt on the spot. And she still had to get on the bike and sit behind him and wrap her arms around his waist. She wasn't sure her brain could be trusted to convey all those messages.

She should have declined his offer, she'd remember that next time.

But it was too late now. She'd been on a motorbike before. It was probably no different from cycling—it would all come back to her once she got on. Her ex had a trail bike that he'd used to ride around his parents' property and to school. He would pick her up every morning and give her a lift, but they'd been seventeen then. She couldn't remember the last time she'd ridden on the back of his bike, and as she wrapped her arms around Seb's waist and felt his body heat radiating into her she thought she certainly didn't remember feeling like this.

The bike vibrated between her thighs. She pressed her legs into the seat as she held on tight. Her face was tucked against his shoulder blade and she could smell him. He smelt fresh and tangy; there was a trace of citrus in his aftershave, lime perhaps.

She probably should have walked home but she was glad she hadn't. She was quite happy right where she was.

CHAPTER THREE

LUCI'S MORNING STARTED with orientation at the family and community health clinic attached to North Sydney Hospital. She spent the morning getting her ID, setting up her email and running through the safety policies and procedures for the site. Once the administration side of things had been dealt with, she would start work. The course participants would be given a case load as the service tried to get through their waiting list. The system was under the pump, there were always more people who needed the service.

Her diary showed her running an immunisation clinic. It was an easy, straightforward introduction that didn't require her to have detailed backgrounds or rapport with the clients. She worked steadily through the hours after lunch. She had bumped into Seb once but it seemed that the staff worked autonomously and she was almost able to forget that he was there. Almost.

But all that changed when her two-thirty client didn't keep her appointment. Melanie Parsons had booked her son, Milo, in for his six-month check and immunisations. When she failed to arrive Luci pulled up her file on the computer. There were numerous entries and lots of red flags.

This woman was a victim of domestic violence. Her past medical history included three full-term pregnancies, one miscarriage and a long list of broken bones and medical treatment for bruising and lacerations. And they were only the things she'd consulted a doctor about. Luci would bet her house that there were more incidents that had gone unreported.

Luci picked up the phone and dialled the client's number. The community health centre's policy stated that all no-shows had to be followed up with a phone call. She checked the file again. It was possible that Melanie had just forgotten her appointment or was catching up on some sleep;

it couldn't be easy having three children under the age of five.

But the phone went unanswered.

Luci needed to be able to record a reason for the non-attendance. In instances where that wasn't possible she had been told to let the co-ordinator know. She went to discuss the situation with Gayle, the health centre co-ordinator, to find out what the next step in the process was.

Gayle brought Melanie's notes up in her system.

'Can you discuss this with Dr Hollingsworth?' she suggested. 'He knows Melanie, he's treated her before.'

Luci heard the unspoken words and she'd seen the supporting evidence in Melanie's file. Seb had treated her for injuries sustained at the hands of someone else.

She knocked on Seb's open door.

'Have you got a minute?' she asked. He was entering notes into the computer system. He looked up and smiled. His blue eyes sparkled and Luci felt herself start to blush.

'Sure.'

She stepped inside and closed his door. She didn't want anyone else to overhear the conversation. 'Melanie Parsons. Do you know her?'

Seb nodded. 'Is she here?'

'No. She had an appointment to get her baby's six-month immunisations but she hasn't shown up. Gayle suggested I talk to you about her.'

'Have you called her?'

'Yes. There was no answer.'

'Do you know her history?'

Luci nodded. 'I've read her file.'

'Someone will need to call past her house and check on her. What time do you finish?'

'I don't think I should be the one to do a home visit,' Luci objected. 'She doesn't know me from a bar of soap.' She was not the right person for that particular job. Someone who had already established some rapport with Melanie would be far more suitable.

'I agree. But if our timing is right we can go together. You can immunise the baby and I'll see what's up with Melanie,' Seb replied. He clicked his mouse and opened his diary. 'I should be finished by three-thirty. Let me know if that works for you.'

Seb was waiting at Reception for her when she finished her clinic. 'Do you want me to drive or navigate?' he asked her as he signed out one of the work cars and collected the keys.

'I don't think I'm game to drive on your roads,' Luci replied. The streets of Sydney were narrow, winding and steep, not at all like the wide, straight roads she was used to. 'But I should warn you, my navigating skills might not be much good either as I'm not familiar with Sydney.'

'No worries. I'll get the map up on my phone.' Seb handed her his phone and she followed him out to the car.

It wasn't long before Seb pulled to a stop in front of a squat red-brick house. It had a low wire fence and a front lawn that needed mowing. There was an old station wagon parked under a carport at the side of the house and a couple of kids' bikes were lying abandoned behind the car in the driveway. The house could do with a coat of paint but it looked lived in rather than neglected. Luci had seen plenty of houses just like it in country towns in her district.

The driveway gate squeaked as Seb pushed it open, announcing their arrival. He closed it behind Luci before leading the way up the concrete path to the veranda. He knocked but there was no answer. The screen door was locked but the front door was ajar. Someone was home. Luci could hear the sound of children playing.

'Melanie?' Seb called out. 'It's Dr Hollingsworth. You missed Milo's appointment at the clinic. I need to know that you are okay.'

Through the screen door Luci could see movement in the dark passage. A woman came to the door but didn't unlatch it. She stood, half-hidden behind the door with her face turned away from them to her left.

'Hello, Melanie.' Seb struck up a conversation as if it was perfectly normal to talk through a door. 'Milo was due for his six-month check-up and vaccinations today. This is Luci Dawson.' He lifted a hand and gestured towards Luci. 'She's a nurse at the health centre. Seeing as we're here and you're home, can we come in and see the kids?'

Melanie nodded. She unlocked the door and stepped aside. She was thin. Luci knew they were the same age but Melanie looked older. Her shoulder-length brown hair was lank but her skin was clear. However, Luci didn't really take any of that in. She couldn't when all she could see was Melanie's black eye. Her left eye was slightly swollen and coloured purple with just a hint of green. The bruise looked to be a day or two old.

'Thank you,' Seb said, as he stepped into the hall and reached for Melanie's chin. Luci expected her to flinch or pull away but she didn't. She must trust Seb.

Luci knew Seb had looked after her before. He'd filled her in on his involvement on the drive over here but Luci hadn't anticipated that she would see the evidence of Melanie's husband's abuse for herself. She hadn't been expecting that.

Seb turned Melanie's face to the right.

'You're hurt.'

'I knocked into the corner of the car boot.' Melanie's eyes were downcast.

'I haven't heard that one before.'

'It's nothing. I've had worse. You know I have,' she said, as she turned away and led them into the house. They followed her into a tired-looking sitting room. The arms of the couch were ripped and stained but Melanie had put a sheet over the cushions in an attempt to brighten the room or maybe disguise the state of the furniture. Everything looked well worn and tired. A bit like Melanie.

She collapsed onto the couch and Seb pulled an upright dining chair closer to the couch and sat on it, facing Melanie. 'What was it this time?'

'It's not his fault, Dr Hollingsworth. I'm pregnant again.'

'And how is that not his fault?' Seb's voice was quiet. He wasn't judging her but Luci could tell he was frustrated.

'He says we can't afford more kids.'

'It takes two, Melanie. He can't blame you.'

Melanie kept her eyes downcast. She had her hands in her lap, clenched together, and Luci knew she was close to tears. Luci wanted to tell Seb to let it go but she knew he couldn't. They couldn't ignore what was going on here. She knew from Melanie's file that she already had three kids—Milo, who was six months old, a two-and-a-half-year-old toddler and a four-year-old. That was a handful for anyone, let alone a woman with an abusive partner.

Seb had told her that he had advised Melanie to take her kids and leave. She had left once but had then gone back, making the usual excuses about him being the kids' father and saying that she loved him. Luci knew it was a difficult decision and something that was hard to understand unless you'd been in that position yourself or had worked with victims of domestic violence. The women were often trapped by their circumstances and Luci suspected that would be the case for Melanie. With three kids under five it was unlikely she had time to work, which meant she had no source of income if she left. And potentially no roof over her head either.

Even while Luci realised it wouldn't be easy, she couldn't stop the twinge of jealousy that she felt when she heard that Melanie was pregnant again. Luci would give her right arm for a family.

But she knew she had to put her own issues aside. Her job, their job, was to help Melanie. Luci wanted to jump in, she had suggestions on how to assist Melanie to change her situation, but Seb must have sensed her desire to offer her opinion and he put a stop to it by asking her to do Milo's health check. Did he think Melanie would open up more if she wasn't in the room? He was probably right. Melanie was unlikely to want to discuss her problems in front of a stranger.

'Milo hasn't had a cold or been unwell?' Luci clarified with Melanie. 'Any concerns at all?' she asked, figuring that as Melanie had three children she would know what to look out for by now.

Melanie shook her head. 'He's been fine. He's on baby formula now and some solids. He's in the room across the hall.'

'No ear infections, colds or reaction to any other immunisations?'

'No.'

Luci picked up her nursing bag and crossed the hall and found herself in a child's bedroom. A bunk bed stood against one wall and Milo's cot was in the opposite corner. He was lying in his cot but he was awake. His eyes followed her as she came towards him.

There was a change mat leaning against the cot and she put it on the bottom bunk. She chatted softly to Milo as she lifted him out of the cot. She could smell a dirty nappy. She laid him down and undressed him, removing his nappy and singlet. She needed to check his hips and testes and it would also give her a chance to check for any bruises or other signs of maltreatment. She was relieved to find nothing. His soft baby skin was unmarked and besides his dirty nappy he was perfectly clean and seemingly well cared for. She found a clean nappy and his blue health-care book on a shelf. She changed his nappy and listened to his chest then recorded his length and weight. He was in the average range for both. He seemed like a happy, healthy little boy.

She gave him his oral polio vaccine and then his immunisation injection and then she couldn't resist a cuddle. She took a deep breath, getting her fill of tiny baby smell. He smelt like talcum powder and baby lotion and the smell made her heart ache. She closed her eyes and wondered if coming to Sydney to study family and community health had been the right decision. She'd been so keen to escape Vickers Hill that she hadn't really considered the ramifications of taking the course. She was going to be exposed to plenty of babies and pregnant mothers. Perhaps she should have enrolled in an aged-care course instead.

Milo was grizzling a little after his injection so Luci took him back with her and handed him to his mum. She recorded the details of the vaccinations in the little blue book while she listened to Seb's conversation with Melanie.

'It's worse when he's been drinking,' she was saying.

'Today is Friday. I suppose he'll be going to the

pub after work tonight?' Seb asked. When Melanie nodded he continued, 'Is there someone you could ask to come over? A friend, your mum or a sister? If you are going to stay here then I think it would be wise to have someone else here with you for support when he gets home.'

Melanie wouldn't maintain eye contact and Luci knew she had no intention of following Seb's suggestion.

'Your decision, Melanie,' Seb said as he stood up. Perhaps he realised he was getting nowhere. 'But I will be checking to make sure you keep the appointment that I'll make for you with the counsellor, okay?'

He gathered his things and Luci went with him out to the car.

'We can't just leave her there,' Luci exploded as she clicked her seat belt into position. She'd been fighting to keep her temper under control and had just managed to hold it together until they had some privacy.

'What else do you suggest we do?' Seb asked. 'She doesn't want to leave and when she has left in the past it's never been for long. She always goes back. We have to pick our battles.'

'But she should be thinking about the children.'

'Melanie says he's never hurt them. Did you see anything to indicate otherwise?'

'No.' Luci shook her head. 'Milo was perfectly healthy and happy but still it's no way for those children to grow up. They shouldn't have to see that, plus it perpetuates the cycle of abuse.'

'I know that. Trust me, we're working on it. I will make an appointment for her to see a counsellor. For us to be able to make any real difference we need to support Melanie to find a way out of this. She will need somewhere to live and she will need money. There is new legislation that can force the perpetrator to leave the premises so that the victim can stay in their home, but I'm not convinced that is a workable solution. It makes it far too easy for the abusive party to find the victim. Court orders ordering them to stay away are violated on a regular basis. This is a problem that can't be fixed overnight and it can't be fixed unless Melanie wants it to change, but I promise I will be doing everything I can.'

Luci nodded. 'I'm sorry,' she apologised. She should have guessed Seb would do what he thought was best. 'I jumped down your throat.'

'It's okay. I know it's hard to understand when you're strong and independent how someone else can put up with circumstances that you would never dream of tolerating. But try to see it from Melanie's point of view. She feels she doesn't have any other option. Again it's about education and support. But these things take time. Not everyone can just up and leave. If you want to work in community health you're going to need to have patience and empathy. Don't stop wanting better things for people but don't expect them all to be like you.'

Luci got off her high horse. She knew all that. She didn't have to look too hard to find the similarities between her situation and Melanie's. She understood how much effort and energy and strength it took to leave the familiar. She hadn't left Vickers Hill without a push from Flick, and her circumstances were far better than Melanie's. She'd only had to leave behind an ex-husband— one who had never beaten her, just one who'd decided he wanted a different life. She knew she couldn't be critical of Melanie or Seb.

'Now, let's talk about something else,' Seb said as he turned onto the main road. 'Something happier. What are your plans for the weekend?'

'I should be studying,' she replied, as she tried to put Melanie and her circumstances out of her mind. Seb had said he would monitor the situation and she had to trust him to do that. 'I have an assignment due Monday.'

'How long do you need?'

'I'm not sure. Why?'

Seb shrugged. 'You said you've never been to Sydney before. I have a free day tomorrow. If you like, I could show you around.'

She should get started on her assignment but when faced with a choice between spending her day with a gorgeous tourist guide or her laptop it was a no brainer. If she got started on her assignment tonight she should be able to finish it on Sunday. She'd get it done on time even if it meant staying up all night. She wasn't about to knock back Seb's invitation.

'I'd love that, thank you.'

There was a sticky note from Seb stuck on the kettle. In two days he'd figured out that the first thing she did every morning was switch the kettle on. She smiled as she read the note and waited for the water to boil.

Meet me on the beach at ten a.m. Bring togs, a hat and sunglasses.

Excitement swirled in her belly. She knew she needed to get her assignment finished but she'd just work all day tomorrow. She wasn't going to miss this opportunity for sightseeing or spending time with Seb. In just a couple of days she could already feel herself changing, becoming the person she thought she could be. She was leaving the old Luci behind. Leaving behind the doubts and the failures. This was her time to start again, to step through the doorway and into her future, and it felt like Seb could help open the door.

She slipped a white cotton sundress over her black bikini, sunglasses over her eyes and a soft, straw hat onto her head. Figuring she'd need a towel if she needed her bathers, she stuffed one and some sunscreen into a bag and headed to the beach across the road.

The beach was small, really only a cove, and apart from a couple and their dog it was empty. Luci scanned up and down along the sand but she couldn't see any sign of Seb. Assuming he wouldn't be far, she sat on the sand and looked out to sea. Little boats bobbed on the water at their moorings, but there were a lot fewer than normal. People must have headed out for the day. The weather was perfect for boating, the sky bright blue and cloudless, the water relatively calm, and the sun was already warm.

Movement to her right caught her eye and she watched as a man rowed a dinghy towards the shore. He had his back to her and was bare to the waist, and she watched the muscles in his back flex and relax as he pulled the oars through the water. As the boat got closer she realised the oarsman was Seb. She barely knew him and it wasn't like she could recognise his movement patterns or even the shape of his shoulders and torso yet, but she recognised the funny fluttery feeling in her stomach that she got when he was nearby.

The boat ran aground and he stowed the oars and jumped out in one fluid and graceful movement. He turned and smiled when he saw her waiting there. His hair was wet, it looked darker than his normal chestnut, and his bare chest was lightly tanned and perfectly sculpted. His swimming trunks were damp and clung to his thighs. She swallowed as the fluttery feeling in her stomach intensified.

'Good morning,' he greeted her.

'Good morning,' she replied, hoping the sun was hiding the blush that she could feel stealing over her cheeks.

He reached out a hand and helped her to her feet. His hand was warm and strong but his grip was gentle. The butterflies in her stomach went crazy.

'You're ready?' he asked her.

'Where are we going?'

'Out on the harbour.'

Luci looked doubtfully at the boat at the water's edge. 'In that?'

Was he kidding? The boat was barely ten feet long and had no motor.

'At first.' He was laughing at her discomfort. 'You're not a sailor?'

'I grew up in the country. This looks a little small,' she said, as she stood and surveyed the little vessel.

'It's okay. I have a bigger boat.' He smiled at her and Luci noticed that his eyes were the same bright blue as the sky. 'This is just the tender to get us out there. Hop in.'

He took her bag and held her hand as he helped her into the dinghy. Her body came to life with his touch. The butterflies took flight and swarmed out of her stomach and lodged in her throat. She didn't think she could breathe. But he had to let go of her to push the boat off the beach and then she was able to inhale a lungful of salty sea air.

He spun the boat around and jumped in, sitting on the seat opposite her. Their knees were almost touching.

He gripped the oars and pulled through the water. She could see his muscles straining. His biceps and triceps alternately tensed and relaxed. His pectoral muscles flexed in his chest. His abdominal muscles were taut. She could feel a blush deepening on her cheeks. She looked out at the harbour as she tried to get herself under control.

'What is your boat called?' she asked, as she scanned the yachts, reading the names painted on the hulls.

'She doesn't have a name yet. She needs a bit of work and once she's finished I'll work out what to call her. It will depend on how she feels.'

'She?'

'All boats are female.'

'Why is that?'

'I'm not sure.' He grinned and she suspected he was about to spin her a story. 'Probably because no matter how much money you spend on them, it's never enough.'

'Hey, that's not fair,' she argued, as he laughed. 'We're not all high maintenance.'

'Well, I hope *you're* not because you might be disappointed by today if you are.'

Luci doubted that. In her opinion the day was already off to a very good start.

Seb pulled the dinghy to a stop beside a sleek white cabin cruiser, then secured the tender before stepping on board and reaching for her hand. Luci was prepared for her reaction to his touch this time and managed to take a deep breath before she took his hand. He helped her on board and then picked up a boathook and dragged a mooring rope closer and tied off the tender.

'Come, I'll give you a tour before we take off.'

'A tour?' Of what? she wondered. Surely there wasn't much to see?

He opened a small gate at the rear of the boat and Luci stepped off the back ledge. There was a steering wheel with a driver's seat and a small bench seat ran perpendicular to that along the left-hand side of the boat. Luci knew that left and right weren't called that on a boat but she didn't know much else.

Seb put her bag on the seat. 'Follow me,' he said as he ducked his head and made his way down three small steps into the front of the boat.

Luci hadn't noticed the steps until Seb showed her but she did as she was told, finding herself in a compact cabin. A kitchen bench complete with a sink ran along the wall to her right and a small table surrounded by a bench seat sat to her left. In front of her, at waist height, raised above a bank of cupboards, was a large flat wooden surface. But all of that barely registered. Seb was still shirtless and the small confines of the cabin meant he was standing only inches from her. She realised that he must have swum out to the boat to retrieve the tender before rowing back to shore to collect her. His chest was smooth and almost hairless and she could see the white spots where the salt had dried on his skin.

'This is it.' Seb's head was almost brushing the ceiling and his left hand almost brushed against her as he gestured to the space around them. 'I have to install new kitchen cabinets and appliances, these have seen better days, and...' he slapped his palm a couple of times on the flat wooden platform '...get a decent mattress for my nautical futon and then I'll be able to take her out for more than just day trips.'

'You'll be able to sleep on the boat?'

'I already have but only in my swag. But if I'm going to live on her I want something a little more comfortable and permanent than that.'

'Live on it?'

'That's my plan. There's a bathroom in here, the toilet is working,' he said as he opened a narrow door next to the bed, 'and once the shower is operational and the new kitchen is installed I'm good to go.'

'But it's so small!' Luci looked around. It possibly had everything a man might need but there was no getting away from the fact that it was at the compact end of the scale spectrum.

'Haven't you ever had a holiday in a caravan?'

Luci laughed. 'A holiday, yes, but I'm not sure I'd want to live in a caravan.' *Or on a boat.*

'I've spent plenty of nights in my swag under the stars with just my bike and a camp fire for company. This will be five-star compared to that. And whenever I get tired of one place I can just haul up the anchor and be off.'

Luci didn't want to rain on his parade. It wasn't her place to comment on his choice of accommodation and she supposed it did sound romantic—for a while.

She wondered what it would be like to be so free. She was busy trying to pay off the mortgage on her house and it would be years until she was free of that commitment. But while she could see the appeal of being debt-free, she knew that deep down she would still want a home. She needed that security.

'It sounds like fun,' she said, determined not to be a naysayer.

She looked around. It didn't take long. The boat was only big enough for one person to live on—just. It looked like Seb wasn't planning on sharing it with anyone on a permanent basis and she wondered why. He was a smart, attractive man; he must have women lining up at his door. Why would he choose to hide away on a boat built for one? A boat that for all intents and purposes seemed very much like a bachelor pad?

The tour over, she followed him back up the steps.

'Have a seat,' Seb said, indicating the bench seat to the left of the wheel. 'There are cold drinks in the ice box and life jackets and a bucket under your seat. Fire extinguisher here.' He pointed to a small red cylinder attached to the side of the steering mechanism. 'And that concludes the safety briefing.'

'You're making me nervous.'

'I may not have finished the cosmetic side of things but I promise she's seaworthy,' he said as he pushed a button and the engine roared to life. He released the boat from her mooring, put it into gear and headed out of the cove.

The boat's engine rumbled under her feet and the noise made conversation difficult but Luci didn't care. She stowed her bag beneath her seat and stretched out, enamoured with the view of both scenery and the driver. North Head and South Head jutted out into the ocean to their left. Luci could see a lighthouse on top of South Head and whitecaps on the water of the Pacific Ocean through the rocky outcrops, but Seb veered to the right, staying within the harbour, and followed the Manly ferry on its way to Circular Quay.

Seb pointed out the Prime Minister's house and Taronga Park Zoo as they motored further into the harbour. It was incredibly beautiful. And busy. It seemed like half of Sydney must be out on the harbour but that didn't detract from the experience.

The Opera House blossomed on the foreshore to their left and Seb slowed the boat down as they approached the iconic building. The drop in speed was accompanied by a decrease in engine noise, allowing them to talk normally.

'This is just brilliant. Thank you so much,' she said as Seb took them under the Harbour Bridge. She looked up at the massive steel structure that spanned the harbour. 'Have you walked across it?' she asked.

Seb laughed. 'You know you can drive across it? Or catch a train? Walking across is the sort of thing tourists do.'

'Well, I'm a tourist.'

'Add it to your list. But you might prefer to climb it or the south pylon. You get a pretty good view of the harbour from up there.'

She was disappointed. It didn't sound like Seb would offer to keep her company if she did want to walk across the bridge.

She rummaged in her bag for her phone to take some pictures. She might not get this view again.

'What, no selfie?'

She turned to find he was grinning at her.

'I'm not that photogenic,' she said, but she suspected that he was. It was a good excuse to capture a picture of him. She stepped beside him and held the phone at arm's length. He put his arm around her and she leaned in and snapped a photo of the two of them.

She checked the photo. Still shirtless, Seb was

lean, muscular, gorgeous and definitely highly photogenic. She'd managed to capture the bridge in the background but she doubted anyone could look past Seb. Not that she planned on showing that photo to anybody, it was strictly for her eyes only.

He circled the boat, turning in front of Luna Park and the clown over the entrance gate grinned manically at them as they passed the jetty. Luci could hear kids screaming on the roller-coasters and she hoped he wasn't planning on taking her to the sideshows. She wasn't keen to spend the afternoon surrounded by a bunch of kids. She needed something less stressful than that but thankfully Seb kept going, steering the boat back towards the Opera House.

'Hand me your phone and I'll take a photo of you,' he said as he put the boat into neutral and idled in front of the Opera House.

Luci passed him her phone and Seb looked at the screen. The tiles that covered the sails of the building sparkled and shimmered in the sunlight, blindingly white against the brilliant blue of the sky. Luci shone just as brightly in the foreground.

She was sublime. She'd taken her hat off for the photo and her golden hair glowed. The sun was on her face, the tip of her nose was going slightly pink and her cheeks were flushed from the breeze. Her eyes were hidden behind sunglasses but she was laughing as he pressed the shutter. Her sundress framed her diamond-shaped freckles. He checked the photo, wishing he'd thought to take it on his phone. That way he would have had a copy to keep.

He tried to ignore the stirrings of lust as he put the boat into gear and cruised between Mrs Macquarie's Chair and Fort Denison and headed for Milk Beach. Luci was like a breath of fresh air in his stale world but his world was no place for her. She was gorgeous but she seemed far too delightful and pure for someone as jaded and disillusioned as he was. Too innocent. The women he'd chosen of late had been just as disheartened by life as he was. There had been no agenda other than short-term, mutual satisfaction, no danger of him damaging anyone's fragile psyche. Girls like Luci were not for him. Or, more specifically, he was no good for girls like her.

He cut through the wake of dozens of other boats, powering through the churned-up water that crisscrossed the blue of the ocean with white foam. The harbour looked magnificent and as they rounded Shark Island the mansions of Point Piper and Rose Bay clung to the hills on their right, adding to the picture-perfect view they had from his boat.

Milk Beach came into sight ahead of them and he pulled back on the throttle as he eased the cabin cruiser into the bay. He cut the engine and dropped anchor a hundred metres off the beach. From this spot they could look back towards the Sydney skyline and, as the boat swung around so her bow faced the city, he heard Luci's intake of breath.

'Wow!' She turned to him and smiled. 'Did you park here deliberately?'

The Harbour Bridge rose majestically across their bow.

'I did.' He was pleased with the reaction he'd elicited, it was just what he'd hoped for. 'The view's pretty good, isn't it?'

'It's incredible.'

It was, he thought. Luci was looking across the water to the bridge but he was watching her. 'I thought we could stop here for lunch and a swim,' he said. The small beach was busy with day trippers but he had been careful to anchor his boat away from the few others that were also enjoying a day out, in order to give them some privacy.

He grabbed the ice box and some cushions from the bench seat and took Luci around to the bow of the boat, where there was room to stretch out. He dropped the cushions on the deck, they would need some padding as the fibreglass hull of the boat could get a little uncomfortable after a while.

Luci spread her towel over the cushions and pulled her sundress over her head, revealing a very tiny bikini. Four triangles of black fabric tied together with black ties. His eyes were drawn to the diamond freckles that nestled between the swell of her breasts.

She pulled a tube of sunscreen from her bag and rubbed it into her shoulders and chest. Seb's brain pounded in his head and his heart raced, sending blood rushing through his body into all five of his extremities. He squatted down and took the lid off the ice box, giving himself a minute to regain his composure. He breathed deeply. He could smell the sea air and sunscreen. He thought he could also smell Luci. Fresh and floral. This girl was doing his head in. She was quite unselfconscious, apparently quite comfortable stripping off in front of him. He guessed there was no reason why she should worry. She had no reason to think he wouldn't be able to keep his eyes off her and people showed just as much flesh on Bondi Beach. But seeing her in a tiny bikini was sending his hormones wild. Not that it was her fault.

He was worried now, worried that she might prove irresistible, worried that he could find himself in hot water. She was down to earth, gorgeous, funny and she smelt sensational. And now she was stretched out beside him wearing nothing but a string bikini. He wasn't sure how he was going to be able to keep his hands to himself.

He wasn't sure he wanted to.

Actually, he knew he definitely *didn't* want to but he had no idea what she thought. Maybe she was looking for some fun, maybe she was disillusioned after her divorce and was looking for some short-term satisfaction, but he suspected it was just wishful thinking on his part. He didn't even know how long she'd been divorced. It could be five minutes or five months. She could have sworn off men altogether.

He offered to rub sunscreen onto her back. That was a legitimate way of not keeping his hands to himself and was possibly the best idea he'd had in a long time, along with inviting her out for the day. Her skin was soft and velvety smooth under his fingers. She lifted her hair away from the nape of her neck, getting it out of his way, and he was sorely tempted to press his lips to the knobbly bone at the base of her neck where it met her shoulders.

Instead, he stepped back, opened the ice box and offered her a drink. God knew, he needed something to help him cool off. He passed her a bottle of water. She sipped her water and then lay back, lifting her face to the sun and closing her eyes.

Seb turned back to the ice box and began to assemble a small plate of cheese, crackers and fruit. He was trying to keep busy, to keep his mind on mundane things and off the fact that a very attractive and semi-naked woman was lying inches away from him. He was unaccustomed to feeling this nervous, and to make matters worse Luci appeared completely at ease and unaware of the effect she was having on him. Which was probably just as well.

He could probably learn a thing or two from her. She was relaxed, easygoing and she didn't appear to have let her failed marriage stop her from having fun. She certainly hadn't shut herself off from others, like he had. He knew he had laughed more often and smiled more frequently in the past three days than he had in the past three years. And the only thing that had changed was that Luci had come into his life. He had separated himself socially, his focus had been on his work and his boat for the past three years, and he had kept any interaction with others to a minimum. His chosen response to any invitation was to decline it politely and yet Luci hadn't hesitated to say yes to all three of his invitations—an after-work drink, a lift home on his bike and now a day on his boat.

For a man who had knocked back most opportunities to spend time with other people over the past three years he didn't want to think about why he was suddenly inviting someone into his life. He must be crazy. Maybe his solitary lifestyle was slowly driving him mad.

What was it about Luci that made him feel the need to spend time with her?

He knew what it was. It was the way she made him feel.

Three years ago he'd lost everything, including a large chunk of his heart and soul, but Luci was waking him up again. He'd been holding his breath, marking time, treading water, and now he felt like he could breathe again.

He put the fruit platter into the shade and ran his eyes over her still figure. Her skin was already turning golden in the sun, her breasts were round and firm, her stomach flat, her legs were toned and athletic, and her toenails were painted pale pink.

Luci sat up. Had she felt him staring at her? Maybe, but she didn't seem perturbed.

'This is much more fun than studying,' she said as she sliced a piece of cheese and popped it onto a biscuit. 'I have never spent a day like this before. All the boat trips I've ever been on involved fishing with my dad in the Gulf of St Vincent in a little tinny, much like the one you rowed before. Nothing nearly as fancy as this.'

'Wait until I finish her. Then we'll be talking fancy.'

'Really?'

Seb laughed. 'No. I don't need fancy. She just

has to be comfortable. A decent bed and a fridge and I'll be happy.'

Luci stretched her arms over her head and her breasts lifted. They were barely contained in her minuscule bikini and Seb couldn't help but notice. He was finding it extremely difficult to ignore her. He really was in trouble.

'Poor Callum,' she said with a half sigh as she surveyed their surroundings. 'I wonder what he's up to this weekend. I think he might have drawn the short straw in the house-swap stakes.'

Seb smiled. 'I'm sure he'll be okay.'

'Have you spoken to him?' she asked.

'No. I sent him a text, saying I was in town and that I was crashing at his place—after discussion with you. He replied saying he's not fussed.'

'I hope he's settling in.'

'You said he's working with your dad?'

'Yes. And with my friend Flick.' Luci laughed, a warm, rich sound. 'God, I hope he survives. There'll be plenty of patients inventing illnesses in order to get a look at the new doctor. I hope he's made of stern stuff.'

'You don't need to worry about us Hollingsworths. We're tough.' They were definitely the strong, silent type, masters of putting on a brave face and keeping their own counsel. Sometimes he wasn't sure how they had managed to get through the couple of traumatic events they had faced in their lives but he didn't want to think about those days now. Today was about Luci and he was keen to find out more.

'You haven't spoken to your dad?'

'No, I've spoken briefly to Mum but not Dad. He works such ridiculous hours, I don't like to interrupt unless it's something really important. He's supposed to be retiring this year. I know Mum is looking forward to that. Perhaps they'll finally be able to do some of the things they've been putting off. But, of course, that depends on Dad finding someone to take over the practice. Even though Vickers Hill is only a couple of hours from Adelaide, not everyone wants to work in the country and he won't leave his patients in the lurch.'

'Vickers Hill is north of Adelaide?' Seb asked,

even though he knew the answer. He'd looked it up, intrigued to know where Luci had come from.

Luci nodded. 'Known for its wine. Dad has bought a small acreage and he and Mum are going to grow grapes and have chickens and ducks. That's the plan anyway. I think they should move further away otherwise Dad will find it hard to retire completely. Old patients will still come to him with their troubles if they see him around town but I guess that's for him to sort out.'

'Can you see them leaving?'

'Not really.'

'And what about you? Are you missing home?'

'Not one bit. How can I be missing home when I'm surrounded by this? So far I don't have any regrets about coming to Sydney. I'm going to make the most of my time here.' She looked up at Seb and he wondered if spending time with him qualified as making the most of things. He hoped so. 'I jumped at the chance to come to Sydney. Well, not so much jumped, Flick pushed me, but now that I'm here it seems like it was a really good decision.'

She rolled over onto her stomach and Seb struggled to keep his eyes off her very shapely behind.

'You have no idea how nice it is to just relax and do my own thing, without everyone telling me what they think is best for me. I'm old enough to work that out for myself.'

He did have some idea what it was like to have everyone interfering in his life in what they thought was a helpful way. That's why he loved having the boat. It had been his escape route and he was convinced it had saved his sanity. He'd been able to disappear and avoid talking to anyone.

Luci might profess that she had chosen to take Flick's advice to study interstate but he still thought a large part of her motivation stemmed from having a reason, an excuse, to leave. He still thought she was running away. She might deny it but he recognised the signs. He had seen those same signs in himself. He knew exactly what it was like—he'd been running for three years. He recognised the need to get away from all the people who knew you and your past and your story.

But even though he thought Luci was running away from Vickers Hill he knew he was in no position to judge her for it. He'd shut himself off from the world completely. At least she was still living.

He knew that was the difference between them. For the past three years he hadn't been living. He hadn't thought he was allowed to enjoy life. It hadn't felt right but was it okay? Was it allowed? Did he have to continue to ignore the world?

Possibly. It was the only way to ensure it didn't hurt him again.

But he knew it was going to be hard to ignore Luci.

'And what is it you should be doing?' he asked, continuing the conversation she had started.

'I don't know yet.' She laughed. 'That's a little ironic, isn't it, but it's early days still. I'll figure it out. On my own. My life is different from how I pictured it. I just have to figure out what I want it to be like from now on. And one benefit of being divorced is that I can figure it out for myself. It's up to me.

'What did you think your life would be like?'

She shrugged and averted her eyes. 'Married with kids.'

He supposed that was quite different from being divorced with no kids. 'Your husband didn't want kids?' he asked. Maybe that was why they'd got divorced.

'No, he did. We both did.' Luci was restless. She rolled back over so she was sitting up now. 'But he decided he didn't want them with me.' She stood up and dropped her hat and sunglasses onto her towel. 'I think I might go for a swim.'

It was clear she wanted to avoid this particular conversation. There was obviously more to the story but he wasn't going to push her. It was none of his business. He would listen if she wanted to talk but from what she had already said she was tired of interference. He decided he would just let her be but he wondered about her ex-husband. What sort of man was he? Luci had told him they had been together for almost ten years. What sort of man took that long to decide that he didn't want to be with someone? What sort of man married a girl like Luci and talked about raising a family together, only to leave her right when they should have been starting that future?

Seb felt a sudden surge of anger towards Luci's ex. He wasn't normally a violent man but he could see the hurt in her eyes and hear it in her voice and something within him made him wish he could fix it. But that reaction was out of character for him. He expected other people to leave him alone, not to interfere in his life, and he had learnt to do the same. But he wanted to help her and had no idea what to do.

He suspected she was not over the divorce and not over the loss of her dreams for the future but he had no idea what she needed. He could almost feel steam coming out of his ears and knew he needed to cool down. Calm down.

Luci was treading water a few metres from the boat, looking towards the shore. He dived in after her. He would keep quiet. He was good at that, it was easy not to speak about his thoughts and feelings or anything emotional. He floated on his back and waited to see what Luci would do. After a few minutes she drifted over to him.

'If you weren't messing about in boats when you were growing up, what did you do on week-ends?' he asked.

'Chased the boys,' she replied.

Her mood had shifted, she was happy again. He thought that by nature she was a sunny person and that drew him to her even more. She balanced out his sombre side. He hadn't always been dark but the events of three years ago made him more reserved, less carefree and more sceptical about the good things in life.

'I thought the boys would have been chasing you.'

'There wasn't much chasing going on, if I'm honest. The girls played netball in winter and tennis in summer. The boys played footy and cricket. Our parents tried to keep us busy. We'd ride around town on our bikes and during harvest we'd often lend a hand if we had friends who had vineyards or farms. There was plenty to keep us out of trouble.'

Her stomach rumbled.

'Time for lunch?'

She nodded. 'Swimming always makes me hungry.'

Sex always made him hungry and Luci made him think of sex. Therefore he was hungry too but he didn't mention that.

Luci was looking back at the boat. 'I didn't think that through when I went for a swim.'

'What?'

'How I was going to get back on.'

'Swim to the back, and I'll help you up the ladder.' The ladder was short but it required substantial upper-body strength to haul yourself out of the water. 'I'll go first and give you a hand.'

They swam side by side and when they reached the boat Seb stretched up for the top rung of the ladder and pulled himself up onto the deck.

'Reach up and give me your hand.' He leaned down and grasped her hand in his. 'Grab the ladder with your other hand,' he said as he pulled her up into the boat and into his arms. Luci might not have thought about the logistics of getting back on the boat but Seb hadn't thought about the logistics of helping her. There wasn't much room at the back, just the small ledge. His back was to the gate and to open it he had to turn round and let her go. He didn't want to do that. They were squashed into a space less than a metre square. Her body was soft against his, slick with water. Her skin was cool and he could feel her heart beating in her chest, beating against his.

She looked up at him.

They stared at each other in silence until he could stand it no longer.

He didn't stop to think about what he was doing. He couldn't think. All he could do was see and smell and feel.

He saw her blue-grey eyes looking at him, the freckles dusted across the bridge of her nose, the tip of it turning red with the sun. Saw the pink rosebud of her lips and wanted to taste her.

He couldn't ignore her and he couldn't resist. He bent his head, making his intention clear, waiting for her to tell him to stop. But she remained quiet. He couldn't hear the sound of the ocean or the other bathers. All he could hear was the sound of their breathing, heavy in the stillness. He could see her eyes watching his and then they flicked down to his lips. He knew she understood his intention but she didn't protest and that was all the invitation Seb needed.

CHAPTER FOUR

He bent his head.

Luci lifted her chin, offering her lips to him, and he claimed them. Claimed her.

He kissed her firmly, just like he'd been wanting to.

He pressed his lips to hers. She tasted of salt and she smelt of sunshine.

She parted her lips, opening her mouth to him. His tongue darted inside, tasting her, touching her. He couldn't control his desire. She was irresistible. But while his own lack of control surprised him she surprised him more when she kissed him back. His hands slid down her back and over the bow of her bikini top. With one flick of his fingers he could untie that bow and he would be able to feel the swell of her breasts pressed against him, skin to skin. But this time he did resist. He moved his hands lower until they cupped her buttocks instead. Firm and round, they fitted perfectly into his palms.

He pulled her into him, pressing her against him as he deepened the kiss. Her mouth was warm, soft and inviting. Her body was cool and soft under his hands.

His body was hard and firm and he held himself back. He didn't want to overpower her.

He felt her hands on his chest. They were cool over his racing heart.

She pushed gently against him, pulling away.

She looked up at him. Her blue-grey eyes were enormous, her pupils dilated. She was panting softly. She was out of breath, they both were.

They stood in silence, looking at each other, waiting for someone to say something. He wasn't going to apologise for kissing her. It had been the right time and the right place and she certainly hadn't resisted. But now she looked unsure. Albeit thoroughly kissed.

Her lips were dark pink now, almost red. She didn't look upset. Just uncertain.

He didn't think she wanted an apology. She hadn't objected but now she looked wary.

'Should I stop?' he asked.

She didn't reply immediately. She just stood, wrapped in his arms, staring up at him, and he could almost see her thoughts spinning in her brain, swirling behind her eyes.

'I don't know what you should do. I don't know what *I* should do,' she replied. 'I can't think.'

'Did I make you uncomfortable?' He wasn't going to apologise for kissing her. He wasn't sorry and he didn't think she was either.

'It's not that.' She paused and stepped away. 'But I wasn't expecting it.'

'The kiss?' he asked. He was pretty sure she'd seen it coming.

She shook her head. 'No. How it felt.'

He thought it had been amazing but his heart stopped for a second as he wondered if perhaps she hadn't been quite so astounded. 'And how was that?' he couldn't stop himself from asking. He had to know.

'Different.'

'Good different?' He had never fished for compliments before but he had to know if the kiss had rocked her world in the same way it had his.

'Good *and* different. I don't know if there's such a thing as "good different". I'm not used to different. I think that's the unexpected thing. I'm not used to kissing a man I've just met. I'm not used to kissing anyone except my ex-husband.'

'Really?' That was it? She'd had one relationship?

'Ben and I were together since I was fifteen. I've only been divorced six months.'

In that sentence lay the answers to several of his questions, the first being how long she had been divorced, but the second answer was even more telling. If she'd been ready to move on from her marriage then six months was a reasonable length of time, but if the end of her marriage hadn't been something she'd chosen then a period of readjustment was only normal. She'd said her husband had met someone else. Seb guessed she wasn't ready to do the same. But that didn't preclude them from having some fun. Not if she wanted to. It was all up to her.

'I get it. You need time.'

'Don't get me wrong. It felt good but I don't know if it felt right. I'm not sure what I should be doing. I don't know if I need more time but part of me feels like I should be a bit cautious and the other part is saying just close your eyes and jump.'

'Only you can make that decision,' he said. He wanted her to jump, he desperately wanted her to jump, but he knew that wasn't his call. 'Let me know what you decide. I'm not going to put any pressure on you but I will say this—you're only here for a few weeks. We can enjoy each other's company, no strings attached, no commitment, and then say goodbye. But it's up to you. Think about it. You know where to find me.'

He dropped his arms from around her waist and leaned back to open the gate, allowing them to step into the boat.

They spent the rest of the afternoon talking. Conversation flowed easily, there were no awkward pauses, but the awareness was always there. He could feel the tension in the air around them, crackling and sparking, but they both ignored it. They talked about work, about places he'd visited and her home town; they talked about everything but the kiss they'd shared and where they were going to go from there.

He was serious about his suggestion, though. He was pretty sure she wasn't the one for him long term, it was obvious she wanted to settle down and have a family, something that was definitely not on his agenda, but she was only in town for eight weeks and he was only committed to Sydney for six weeks. There was no reason they couldn't have some fun together. They could enjoy each other's company and then say goodbye. But he would give her space. For now. This had to be her decision.

Luci towelled herself dry and slipped her sundress over her head. She'd had enough time in the sun but the extra layer wasn't to prevent sunburn, it was to provide her with a bit of a barrier. Not that it afforded much protection but she needed all help she could get to ensure she didn't just throw herself back into Seb's arms.

She should be having doubts and reservations. She had known him for less than three days and she had *never* kissed a man she barely knew before. She'd never properly kissed anyone other than her ex-husband.

She should be having doubts and reservations about kissing him, full stop, but that wasn't the issue. It wasn't Seb who was making her nervous but the consequences of her actions.

She didn't want to make a mistake or do anything that might jeopardise her time in Sydney. There were more important things than kissing a handsome stranger. They had to live together and work together. There were a whole lot of reasons why she should keep her distance and only one thing, her hormones, was telling her differently.

She was a single adult, there was no rule saying she couldn't take this further, but she really wasn't sure if she was ready. She needed some

ground rules. She'd never done 'no strings attached' and she wasn't sure if she could. Until
she had processed the idea she felt it would be
wise to keep her distance.

The kiss had been amazing. She'd seen it
coming and she hadn't stopped him. She hadn't
wanted to. She'd wanted to touch him, to taste
him, but she hadn't realised how hard it would
make it to deny herself more. It was going to be
difficult. She would have to find other ways of
keeping busy. If she was busy she wouldn't have
time to think about him.

Seb had pulled some more food out of the ice
box and assembled a picnic lunch. Luci was
starving and she was more than happy to sample
the selection. While she was eating she couldn't
talk but when they did talk Seb kept the conversation neutral. They talked about inconsequen-
tial things, a polite conversation between two
virtual strangers, skirting around the issue that
she couldn't stop thinking about.

But not talking about the kiss didn't stop her
from thinking about it.

* * *

Seb shoved the crowbar behind the last of the kitchen cabinets in the galley of his boat. He had spent most of his spare time for the past week hunkered down, removing the shower and the kitchen cabinetry. The carpenter had told him not to expect the new fittings to be ready for installation for another fortnight but he needed to dismantle the old fixtures and he needed to keep himself occupied.

The demolition work was achieving three things—he was progressing nicely with his renovations, he was keeping his mind occupied, to a point, and he was keeping his distance from Luci. He had promised to give her time and space but over the past couple of days he'd found that if he spent too much time in the same space as her it was becoming increasingly difficult to resist the pull of attraction. It was difficult to be around her and not touch her. All he wanted to do when she was around him was to explore their attraction but he had promised not to push her.

Once again his boat was his sanctuary but this time he didn't need it to help him over his heartbreak. This time it was to keep his mind off his desire rather than his despair. The physical work was a good antidote for the desire. He was so knackered by the end of the day that he would fall straight to sleep when he went to bed. That was a fourth benefit of the demolition work.

He'd had several brief affairs over the past three years but he had been very careful to avoid meaningful relationships. If Luci was willing there was nothing stopping them from having some fun, as her time in Sydney was limited anyway, but he realised she might still be working through her own issues. It would probably be wise to spend some time working out whether her issues were major or minor. He wasn't prepared to get involved in anything too emotional—a physical relationship was fine but he didn't want anything more serious than that.

There were all sorts of reasons why he should

avoid Luci and he knew them all, he'd been running over them constantly.

She had led a sheltered life. A *very* sheltered life.

They had to work together.

They had to *live* together.

It was all a little bit too close.

But that didn't alter the fact that he was excited by Luci and it had been a long time since he'd been excited by anything.

Although he knew it still might be better to avoid her he couldn't avoid her completely. They had to work together and on Friday afternoon she knocked on his consulting-room door. He could smell her before he saw her. She smelt of frangipani.

'Hi,' he said as he looked up. 'How's it going?'

'Good.'

She smiled at him and her blue-grey eyes sparkled. She looked happy. She glowed and he had the sense that she was filled with light that then spilled out to brighten everyone else's day. At least, that's how he felt when she was around.

'Melanie Parsons is in the clinic today,' Luci told him. 'She has an appointment with the psychologist and then I'm going to do the health check on her four-year-old. I wasn't sure if you wanted to see her.'

'Good idea. What time is she booked in with you?' he asked as he looked at his diary.

'She's next. I'm just going to grab a coffee and by then she should be done with the psych consult. Give me ten minutes to get started on the toddler check and then come in.'

Luci was just helping Harper down from the exam table when Seb knocked on the door. She took Harper out of the room to the play area where Harper's two-year-old brother was busy with the building blocks while Seb caught up with Melanie. When she returned Seb had been given the update on the two psychologist appointments Melanie had already had.

'We are working on my responses so that I can try to manage the situation,' Melanie told him. 'And then we're going to tackle the best way to get Brad in for a session as well.'

Milo was strapped into his pram in the corner of the room. He started to grizzle.

'Sorry,' Melanie apologised, 'He's due for a feed.'

Seb thought it was interesting that Melanie felt she needed to apologise for something that was perfectly understandable. She started to get out of her chair to attend to the baby when Luci offered her help.

'Don't worry about him. I'll see if I can settle him for a bit, let you finish with Dr Hollingsworth.' Luci lifted Milo out of the stroller. She blew a raspberry on his foot and his grizzles stopped, becoming happy chortling instead. She laid him on the exam table and distracted him with a mirror and a game of peek-a-boo, allowing Melanie to continue.

The young mother was watching Luci play with Milo while she spoke to Seb. 'And I think I need to make an appointment to discuss a more reliable form of contraception. After this next one I reckon I'm done. Some days I feel like I'm not even managing with the three I already have.'

Seb's antennae went up. 'I'll speak to the psychologist and recommend that you continue with regular visits until a few months after this next baby is born.' He didn't want to let Melanie slip through the cracks in the system. If she needed help and support he wanted to make sure she got it. For her sake and for her children's sake.

'Thank you,' she replied with a nod as she stood up, preparing to leave. She picked Milo up from the exam table to put him back into his stroller. 'Do you have kids, Luci?' she asked.

Melanie was bending over, strapping Milo into his pram, and she missed Luci's expression. But Seb didn't. She looked like someone had slapped her.

'No, I don't,' Luci replied.

'You should. You're a natural.'

'Mmm-hmm.' Luci turned away and Seb wasn't able to see her face. He couldn't tell if her expression had changed or not.

'I don't seem to have the energy,' Melanie remarked.

'I imagine managing them twenty-four-seven is

very different from seeing them for ten minutes at a time,' Luci said. 'I'm not surprised you're tired.'

'Exhausted is the word, I think. But I'll get through it. What other choice do I have?' she remarked as she pushed the pram towards the door.

'Are you okay?' Seb asked Luci the moment Melanie left the room.

'I'm fine.'

She didn't look fine.

'I'm concerned about Melanie, though,' she said, changing the subject. 'Do you still think the kids are safe?'

'How was Harper's health check?' he asked, letting her change of topic go—for now. 'Were there any red flags with her weight or teeth or any unexplained bruises?'

Luci shook her head. 'Everything was within normal ranges.'

'I've never seen any signs of neglect or abuse. The kids are clean and well fed. I think she's coping. Maybe just, at times, but I don't think the kids are in any danger.' If he thought the children were in any danger he wouldn't sit on his hands. 'Her kids' welfare comes before her own, which is part of the problem, but also why I'll insist that she continue with regular psych reviews. If anything changes, hopefully we'll pick up on it.'

Luci was nodding but she still looked upset. He felt that he'd learned to read her expressions in just a few days and he was still worried about her. He wanted to find out why she'd looked so shocked. He ignored his self-imposed ban. He wanted to spend time with her. 'Have you got plans tonight?' he asked.

'Only to cook up a stir-fry.'

'Would there be enough for two?'

'You'll be home?'

So she'd noticed that he'd been MIA. He wondered if she had missed him. He nodded and offered, 'I'll bring wine.'

'Sure.'

'Dinner smells good.'

Seb's voice startled her and made Luci jump. She had her head over the wok and the sizzle as she fried the garlic and crushed chilli had blocked out all other sounds.

'It's just chicken and noodles,' she said as she scraped the marinated chicken strips into the pan. The aroma of fried garlic always smelt good but she hadn't really thought about the practicalities of serving up a dish laden with garlic. Oh, well, she supposed it was one way to make sure Seb didn't kiss her again.

She glanced over her shoulder when she heard the familiar snap as Seb broke the seal on the screw top on the bottle of wine he held. He poured two glasses and handed one to her before leaning back on the kitchen bench.

Was he planning on hanging around in the kitchen while she cooked?

She'd been surprised that he was free tonight. He'd barely been home all week. She'd heard him come in late at night but he definitely hadn't been home for a meal and she'd expected he would have other plans. She'd wondered if he had been deliberately avoiding her and had thought about shooing him out of the kitchen now, but dinner would only take five minutes so she may as well enjoy his company. Sitting home alone was no fun.

The house had been far too quiet this week without Seb. She still wasn't used to being on her own. After her divorce she'd formed a habit of eating at her parents' house a couple of times a week or sharing a meal with Flick. But being in Sydney, where she didn't have a large network of friends, had made her nights long and lonely. She'd never really been on her own before and she'd discovered she didn't like it. But that didn't mean she was going to fall for the first guy to cross her path. She needed to develop some resistance along with her independence.

She sipped her wine, hoping it would calm her nerves. It felt like they were on a date. Not that she really knew how that felt. She and Ben had been together since high school and she couldn't even remember their first date, but she guessed it would have been at a school friend's birthday party. They had probably played silly party games and drunk some wine they'd pinched from a parent's cellar.

She wished she was cooking something a bit more complicated than a stir-fry, something that required more attention. Something that would require her focus but, as it was, she could whip up a stir-fry blindfolded and that meant she had plenty of time to think about Seb.

Even though she hadn't seen much of him that week she could always tell when he'd been to the apartment. She could smell him. The air was different and even now, despite the aroma of garlic and chilli, she could still smell him. He had showered after work—that must have been while she'd been at the supermarket—and she could smell soap and aftershave. He'd changed into a pair of stone-coloured shorts with a fresh navy T-shirt. His feet were bare and he looked relaxed and comfortable. He certainly didn't look nervous or like he was dressed for a date.

Luci took another sip of wine and concentrated on copying Seb's calm approach as she served up the stir-fry and sat at the table opposite him.

He tucked into the bowl of noodles, scooping up several forkfuls before he paused to take a breath.

'This tastes great, thank you,' he said, as he topped up their wine glasses.

Luci had intended to do some studying after dinner but she could fast see that plan disappearing if she had too much wine but she didn't refuse the top-up. After a week of lonely nights it made a pleasant change to share a meal with someone. And it was even more pleasant when that someone was Seb.

'Two weeks down, how's it been going?' he asked her as he sipped his wine. 'Have you recovered from Melanie's visit?'

'What do you mean?'

'Something she said upset you.'

'You noticed that?'

'I did. What was it?'

'I know she didn't mean any harm but if I had a dollar for every time someone asked me if I had kids I'd have paid off my mortgage. I just don't understand why so many clients feel they have a right to ask personal questions.'

'I think she thought you were a natural with kids. She meant it as a compliment.'

'I realise that but I didn't expect that every second person would ask me if I have children. I bet they don't ask you the same thing, do they?'

'Some do,' he admitted, 'but I guess it probably is more of a question between women.'

'They all seem to assume that if a woman is working in family health or paediatrics or obstetrics she would either have kids or want them.'

'But you do want them.'

'Yes, but I don't want to think about it all the time. Obviously my divorce has changed my plans somewhat. I'm not exactly in a position to start a family but I don't want to tell clients my life story.'

'Fair enough.'

'I guess I hadn't anticipated that the subject of children would be raised so often. I need to find an answer to the most popular question, which is, "So, Luci, do you have children?"'

'Why don't you just tell them that you're only young? You've got plenty of time.'

It wasn't a bad suggestion. It wasn't Seb's fault that time wasn't on her side but he didn't know that.

'A lot of these mothers are younger than me. I don't want them to feel I'm judging them. If I had my way I *would* have had children by now. All I've wanted, all my life, was to have kids and to be a young mum. My parents are old. Dad is almost seventy and Mum is a couple of years younger. They are wonderful parents but growing up I really noticed their age. Especially in my town where so many people start their families young, my parents could have been my grandparents and I didn't want to be like that. I also want more than one child. I was an only child and I didn't want that for my kids. Having a family has been my dream since I was a teenager.'

'Why don't you tell them you're waiting for the right man, then?' He scooped up the last mouthful of his dinner and didn't speak again until he'd finished it. 'Or do you think you had the right one in Ben?'

'Obviously I did when I married him.' She had thought that was it for her. As far as she'd been concerned, her life had been sorted when she'd walked down the aisle and become a wife. Until she'd found that it could easily be unsorted.

Ben couldn't have been the right man for her. If he had been, surely they'd still be together? Or perhaps she just wasn't the right woman for him. But when they'd got married she hadn't known what else was out there. Neither of them had. Ben had found someone he felt suited him better and Luci had to hope that there was someone else out there for her too.

What would her perfect man be like?

She looked across the table. She suspected he would be a lot like Seb. That was dangerous territory. She needed a change of topic. A safer direction. 'How was your week?' she asked. 'I barely saw you. Have you changed your mind about sharing the house?'

'No. I wanted to give you some space. Being

around you was testing my limits. It's been difficult to put you in the "friend" zone so I thought it would be best if I stayed out of the way. I've been working on my boat.'

Hearing Seb put their situation like that made her wonder if she wanted to be in the 'friend' zone. She didn't think she did but she was still confused about what she should be doing. It was still safer not to do anything. He hadn't apologised for kissing her. She was glad about that. The kiss had been good, she didn't want an apology, but she wasn't ready to revisit it either.

He was looking at her so directly but she couldn't respond. It was safer not to reply to his comment. To break eye contact, she stood and picked up their empty bowls, clearing the table. She took the bowls to the sink and rinsed them, keeping her back to Seb.

'You don't need to stay out of the house, that doesn't seem fair.' She found her voice once she wasn't looking at him.

'I thought it was easiest for both of us. I promised I wouldn't make you uncomfortable.'

'I'm not uncomfortable. I just can't jump into another relationship.' Even though she was tempted. 'I know I should spread my wings but jumping into something with the first man who crosses my path doesn't really fit that. I think I need to test the water. I've never even been on a proper first date. Maybe I should be the one who spends more time out of the house. Maybe I should meet some more people.'

Seb had been hoping to hear Luci say she'd made a decision. His ego had let him believe that if he gave her time and space she'd miss him. But perhaps she had a point. Perhaps she *did* need to meet other people. Perhaps then she would see that he could be the perfect person with whom to test the water.

But maybe he had a solution to this dilemma.

'I've been invited to a dinner party tomorrow night. If you'd like to come with me it would give you a chance to meet some other people.'

He hadn't actually thought about going until just now. The whole premise of the evening

hadn't appealed to him but now, with Luci's pro-
visos, it was suddenly more attractive.

When Ginny had invited him he'd declined the
invitation. That had become his habit over the
past three years but he knew Ginny wouldn't
mind a last-minute change of mind. They had
been friends since high school and she had made
a lot of effort to keep in contact, especially re-
cently. Even when Seb had been difficult and un-
sociable, Ginny had kept him in the loop, inviting
him to parties and functions. He'd declined almost all of her invitations but he appreciated the
fact that she hadn't given up on him. Perhaps it
was time he said yes.

'Like a date?' Luci queried.

CHAPTER FIVE

'NOT EXACTLY.' HE wished he could offer to take
her on a proper first date but if she was going
to insist on meeting other people then tomorrow
night's party would be a good compromise. If
everything went according to his plan he could
organise a first date after that. 'A friend of mine
is hosting a "dates with mates" party. It's for sin-
gles. Each guest is expected to bring a partner
who they are not romantically involved with—
it's a way of meeting new people, of broaden-
ing your set of acquaintances and potentially
meeting someone who you could date. So it fits
within your rules. We'd be going as friends and
you'll get to meet new people. What do you
think?'

She nodded. 'Sure. I'd like that.'

He was surprised by her immediate reaction.

There was no hesitation, no further questions. She was far more adventurous and sociable than he was.

Luci pulled her hair into a sleek ponytail and applied a coat of pale pink lipstick before zipping herself into the strapless black jumpsuit she'd bought that day. She'd seen it in a shop window that she passed on her way to work and had loved it but had had no reason to buy it. Until today. She'd told herself she hadn't bought anything new in ages so it was a justified purchase. She told herself a lot of things. That she wasn't looking forward to the date, that it wasn't really a date and that she was keen to meet other people when, in fact, she was nervous about pretty much all of it. She was nervous about whether or not she looked okay, whether she'd fit in to the crowd, whether Seb would like her outfit, and what he would be thinking about their 'non-date'.

Seb looked her up and down when she joined him in the lounge room. 'Wow. You look sensational.' Luci relaxed. At least now she knew what he was thinking. 'I was going to suggest we take my bike but perhaps we should call a cab.'

'The bike is fine,' she replied. She enjoyed going on the bike. It gave her a chance to wrap her arms around him and hold on tight. What wasn't to like about that? 'Just let me grab my boots.' She swapped her gladiator sandals for her old work boots and carried her sandals down the stairs to put on when they reached the party. Seb unlocked the compartment under the seat of his motorbike and pulled out his spare helmet, exchanging the helmet for Luci's sandals and the wine. He had his spare jacket tucked under his arm and he held it for her while she slipped her arms in before helping her to fasten her helmet.

He started the bike and Luci straddled the seat behind him. She wrapped her arms around his waist and held on tightly as he rode through the streets of the North Shore to Cremorne Point. He parked his bike on the road behind the house and helped Luci off. She changed her shoes and checked her hair in the mirror, then took a deep breath. She'd come up with the idea of meeting new people but the reality of walking into a party where she knew just one person was more daunting than she would have thought. It was another new situation for her. Something else she'd never done.

Seb took her hand and squeezed it. He must have known she was nervous but having him hold her hand only intensified the feeling. At the same time it felt so good that she didn't want to object.

The party was already under way and music filled the night air. Seb opened the back gate and led her along a narrow path that followed the side of the house. When they emerged into the front garden Luci caught her breath. The house sat right on the harbour and the view was incredible. A white, open-sided marquee had been erected in the centre of the lawn with a dining table positioned beneath it, and closer to the water's edge Luci could see a long bar, loaded with glasses and drinks, that framed the view across the harbour to the Opera House and the bridge.

The garden was lit with hundreds of lights—fairy-lights, up-lights and down-lights—and the

Opera House glowed as the sun set. It looked spectacular.

Ginny came to greet them and Seb introduced her.

'Welcome,' Ginny said, and she kissed Luci on both cheeks. 'I'm so glad you agreed to come. It's been ages since I've seen Seb and I was afraid he was going to turn down this invitation too.'

'Thank you for including me,' Luci said as she gestured to the garden. 'This looks amazing.'

'Thanks but I can't take all the credit. The decorating is my work. I'm a food stylist by trade, but the house belongs to another friend of mine—Michael. Come with me, I'll introduce you.'

Seb and Luci followed Ginny across the lawn to the bar where the other guests had gathered and Luci tried to keep track of who was who during a whirlwind introduction. First up was Paulo, a Spanish chef, who Ginny had met on an assignment. She introduced him with the comment, 'I can make food look pretty but I can't cook so I invited Paulo.' Then there was Michael, who owned the house, and he was followed by a model, a footballer, a massage therapist, Ginny's brother, who worked in finance, a lawyer he knew, an actor and a food blogger. Luci was unsure what a food blogger actually did but the woman was extraordinarily thin so Luci assumed it didn't actually involve eating. It was an interesting assortment of people and Luci thought the evening would either be a lot of fun or a huge disaster.

Ginny had a seating plan arranged and they were told it would change between each course. Luci started the night between Paulo, the Spanish chef, and Michael, her host.

Michael was smooth, dark and good-looking, with a European heritage, Luci suspected. Besides this gorgeous house, he also owned three restaurants. A fact he successfully mentioned within the first few minutes and several times thereafter. He seemed to think Luci should be suitably impressed. She was, but not by him. He was obviously wealthy but that wasn't high on Luci's list of priorities. He also had a very high opinion of himself but no sense of humour. Luci preferred someone who could make her laugh and would let her be herself. She suspected Michael was not that sort of man. She wasn't interested in material objects. She wanted a family and she would give up everything else if she could have that. Nothing else was that important.

Paulo, to her left, was outrageously handsome and quite charming but he wasn't her type of man either. He didn't make her heart race or her breath catch in her throat. He didn't give her the fluttery feeling she got in her stomach whenever Seb was near. If nothing else, this dinner party was helping her to narrow down her type of man.

Somehow she managed to survive the first course and conversations that she wasn't particularly interested in. For the main course she found herself sitting between the actor and the footballer, a rugby league player. He had limited conversation, appearing to be restricted to the topics of rugby and golf, neither of which Luci knew anything about. Her mind drifted to the opposite side of the table where Seb was now seated. She never seemed to have any difficulty talking to him. They had discussed all manner of topics.

She turned her attention to the actor on her other side, leaving the rugby player to try to strike up a conversation with the girl on his right. The actor turned out to be 'between jobs' and working as a barista and he was pleasant enough, although she was pretty sure he was gay. Not that it mattered as she wasn't interested in him anyway, but she wondered who had invited him.

Somehow, through all the various seat changes and movements, she managed to keep one eye on Seb and hoped no one noticed. She thought she was being subtle but it was hard to know. She did her best to concentrate on what the other guests were talking about but as the evening wore on she found it increasingly difficult. All she wanted to do was to swap seats and plonk herself next to Seb.

Even though he made her feel nervous, Luci knew it was the right kind of nervous. The exciting kind. The possibility that something could happen if she was willing. She wondered what the rules were if you decided that the mate you came with was the same one you wanted to go home with. So far, in her opinion, no one could compare to Seb. He didn't need to be the perfect man, it didn't even matter if he was the first one to cross her path, she just knew that she wasn't going to get him out of her system without exploring the possibilities.

If she was honest she'd admit—to him and to herself—that she'd thought about little else for the last week. She didn't want to live in the past. Her marriage was over and at some point she was going to have to try again. And she was more than happy to try again with Seb.

She looked across the table and found him watching her. She blushed and hoped he couldn't read her thoughts. No. It was time to share those thoughts. If she wanted to be a grown-up she had to take the leap. She wanted to stretch her wings and she hoped Seb would give her the opportunity to do just that.

She smiled at him and stood up as dessert was cleared away. Guests gathered in smaller clusters as coffee was served in the garden but before Luci could make her way to Seb she was cornered by Michael. At the beginning of the evening she had thought the evening would either be interesting or a disaster. It looked like it was heading down the path of complete disaster.

She stood patiently for another few minutes as Michael talked some more about himself. She searched the crowd for Seb as she waited for a polite time to escape. Seb was on the other side of the garden, talking to the model who was Ginny's brother's date. Their eyes locked and Michael and his conversation receded into the background. Why was she wasting time with him?

'Would you excuse me?' she said.

She saw Seb break away from the model at the same time. He was coming for her. Luci waited and fell into step beside him, following him in silence down to a wooden garden seat that sat at the harbour's edge.

Finally it was just the two of them.

As she sat next to him her thigh brushed his leg and she wondered if she should move, if he needed some space. But she didn't want to move, so she stayed put. The now familiar butterflies careened around in her stomach. She wanted to touch Seb. Wanted to feel him.

A light breeze blew off the harbour, sending a shiver through Luci.

'Would you like my jacket?' Seb offered.

'No, I'm okay.'

He put his arm around her shoulders and pulled her into his side. He was warm and solid and Luci wanted to close her eyes and soak up the feeling of being in his arms again.

'Are you having fun?' he asked her.

'Not really,' she replied. 'The rugby player is boring, Michael is only interested in himself and Paulo was nice but a bit too smooth for me.'

'Too smooth? I wouldn't have thought that was a thing.'

'It most certainly is, and I think the barista-slash-actor is gay.'

'Really?'

'Yep.'

Seb laughed.

'Why is that funny?' Luci asked.

'It means there's one less bloke in the running.'

'In the running for what?'

'For your attention.'

Luci hesitated for a fraction of a second, wondering if she should tell him what she thought. She decided she should. 'It doesn't matter. I've found the one.'

'Ginny's brother?'

'No. Not him.'

'There isn't anyone else.'

'Yes, there is, but I'm not sure if it's within the rules of the night. Are you allowed to go home with the same person you came with?'

'Go home with? As in together?'

She nodded.

'Are you serious?'

She nodded again. 'As long as it's not against the rules.'

'I don't give a damn about the rules,' Seb said as he stood and reached for her hand. 'Let's get out of here.'

They barely stopped to say thank you and

goodnight to Ginny before making a beeline for Seb's bike. Luci ignored Ginny's knowing smile. She didn't care what anyone thought. What happened between her and Seb was their business, no one else's. Luci was going to do exactly what she wanted for a change and if anyone tried to tell her it was a bad idea she wasn't going to listen.

She slid her hand under Seb's shirt as she sat behind him on the bike. She rested her hand against his chest and imagined what the rest of the night would be like.

They barely made it up the stairs and into the apartment before their clothes started coming off.

Seb kicked off his boots and Luci did the same with hers. He tossed his leather jacket on the floor and pulled his shirt over his head, discarding items of clothing on the passage floor. Luci's jacket followed.

He lifted her up and she wrapped her legs around his waist as he pushed her against the passage wall. He bent his head and kissed her. She opened her mouth and kissed him back.

Her hands were pressed into his shoulder

blades. His skin was firm and smooth. He looked as though he'd been carved from marble but he was warm and pulsing with life. He carried her further into the apartment and she could feel his erection pressing between her thighs.

'Your room or mine?' he asked.

'Yours. It's closer.' Luci didn't think she could wait much longer.

He put her down and reached behind her to unzip her jumpsuit.

'The zip is on the side.'

His hands found the zip and he bent his head as her jumpsuit fell away and pressed his lips against the diamond-shaped freckles on her chest.

'I've wanted to do that since the first time I saw you.'

His fingers brushed over her breasts as he released her bra. He cupped one breast in his hand as he took the other into his mouth, making Luci think she might burst into flames.

She reached for his waistband and unzipped his trousers, discarding them on the floor along with her outfit.

Seb scooped her up and laid her on the bed. His boxer shorts joined his trousers as Luci admired him.

The marble angel in all his glory. His chest was broad and tanned from hours on his boat. Her eyes followed the line of his sternum where it divided his pecs, down to the ridges of his abdominals. Below his belly button a light trail of hair led her eyes further to where his erection was proudly displayed. He was absolutely gorgeous. Perfectly sculpted and ready and waiting for her.

She swallowed feeling moisture pooling between her thighs. She hooked her fingers under the elastic of her knickers, wanting to discard them, but Seb leaned forward and moved her hands. He lifted her hips and gently tugged her underwear down. His fingers brushed the backs of her legs and she felt like she might explode right now. He slid her knickers down over her calves and dropped them on the floor.

Now they were both naked but Luci didn't have time to feel self-conscious. She wasn't thinking about how she looked, she could only focus on how Seb made her feel.

He knelt at the foot of the bed and spread her legs, pushing her knees gently apart. He ran his tongue along the inside of her thigh, starting at her knee. He kept moving up and Luci lifted her hips as his tongue delved and flicked and tasted her.

She reached for him and pulled him up onto the bed. He knelt between her thighs and she circled his erection with her hand, running her thumb over the tip of his shaft. Felt him quiver.

He bent his head and took her breast in his mouth. His tongue was hard and wet as it flicked over her nipple. Luci moaned and arched her back. It had been months since she had felt this way, and couldn't wait any longer.

'Take me now, Seb,' she begged. The tension of the last few days made her impatient. There would be time later to explore, but right now she needed release.

He reached into the bedside drawer and handed her a condom. Luci tore the packet open and rolled it onto him before guiding him into her. She lifted her hips and let him fill her.

She met his thrusts, timing them with her own. She had to learn a new rhythm, faster and harder. He consumed her and she let him.

CHAPTER SIX

SHE CRIED OUT as she came and felt him shudder as he joined her.

It was different.

But good.

There was such a thing as good different after all.

They had made love fast and impatiently, unable to restrain themselves, and then they made love slowly, getting to know every inch of each other. Luci was adventurous and brave as she discovered the joys of sex with Seb. There was no routine, there was no expectation or pressure. It was all new and exciting.

Luci could remember when sex had been like that—when she and Ben hadn't been able to get enough of each other. When they had been young and first married they had grabbed every opportunity and then again when they'd decided it was time to start a family. She'd had plenty of sex but somewhere along the line it had lost the fun and become a chore. At some point it had become another thing on the list of jobs that had to be done.

She knew when that had happened. When, month after month, her dreams of falling pregnant hadn't eventuated. She'd started worrying, constantly taking her temperature, changing her diet, insisting on sex on certain days of the month, certain times of the day—and it had taken the fun out of it. Was it any wonder Ben had started looking elsewhere? She'd blamed him for destroying their marriage single-handedly when the reality was that she'd played her part too.

Remembering how much fun sex could be cheered her up immensely. She still knew how to enjoy life.

She smiled as Seb tucked her in to his side and trailed his finger down her arm. The night hadn't been a complete disaster after all.

'So how was the water?' Seb asked, as his fingers ran over her hip bone and down to the top of her thigh.

Luci's brain had turned to mush. 'Pardon?'

'The water?' Seb repeated. 'You wanted to dip your toe in. I want to know if it was to your liking.'

Luci grinned. 'Very much so. I've decided there is such a thing as good different. But this is all new to me. I need some guidelines.'

'What do you mean?'

'I need to know if we are dating or just having sex.'

'What do you want?'

'I need to have some fun but I also want to see what dating is like in the modern day. When I leave Sydney I need to know what to expect. I need some practice.'

'I think you'll find you'll be fine. Trust me,' he said. 'But I'm happy to be of service for the next four weeks while I'm still here. We can have fun until I leave or until you get sick of me.'

Luci appreciated the fact that he didn't suggest he'd get tired of her first.

'But I do have one condition,' Seb added.

'What's that?'

'We are exclusive while it lasts. No dating anyone else.'

Luci nodded. She had no intention of looking elsewhere. She couldn't imagine needing to.

'So when Michael calls and asks you out, you'd better have an excuse ready.'

'Really? Michael? I thought I made it perfectly clear that I wasn't interested.'

'For some men that only makes you more appealing. For some it's all about the chase. I can see I have a lot to teach you,' he said, as he kissed her shoulder. 'So much to do and so little time.'

'Where do you want to start?' Luci replied with a smile.

'How about we start with this?' he said, flipping her onto her back and ducking his head under the covers.

Luci closed her eyes and gave herself up to him. There was no room in her head for thoughts of anything other than the waves of pleasure that consumed her.

Seb knew exactly what he was doing. This might just be the best decision she had ever made.

Seb woke her in the morning in the same way he'd said goodnight, then got up to make her a cup of tea.

'We might be going about this a little backwards but I have a first date planned,' he said as she sat up in bed and took the tea.

'Now?'

'You might have time for a shower.' He grinned.

The shower took a little longer than normal. Having Seb in there with her, offering to wash her back, wasn't necessarily the timesaver one might expect.

She dressed in jeans, canvas sneakers, a T-shirt and Seb's spare leather jacket and climbed on the back of his bike. Her thighs complained as she stretched them over the seat but she wasn't complaining. She might be a bit stiff and sore but it was an ache she was more than happy to put up with.

'Where are we going?' she asked.

'I'm taking you out for breakfast.'

That sounded good. She was starving.

Seb rode to Milson's Point on the north shore and pulled into a parking spot beside the harbour bridge. There were numerous cafés along the opposite side of the street and Luci wondered which one he had chosen, but Seb didn't cross the street. Instead, he took her hand and led her along the ramparts of the bridge and up a flight of stairs.

'You're going to walk across the bridge with me?' Luci asked as they reached the top and she found herself on the pedestrian walkway that ran along the eastern side of the bridge. 'I thought this was the sort of thing only tourists did?' she teased.

'I figured you're worth making an exception for. But if I'm going to do this then this is the best time of day. It's quiet enough on a Sunday morning to still be relatively peaceful. We can take our time and we'll have breakfast at the other end.'

The view was spectacular, better than Luci had imagined. The Opera House, the botanic gardens and the city skyline were laid out before them as they headed south across the bridge. The sun was still low in the sky to their left and the Opera House sparkled like a sugar-coated meringue on the edge of the harbour. She'd seen it from the water, in daylight and at night-time and now from a higher vantage point. It didn't disappoint, no matter what. She thought it was an incredible building and she knew it would always remind her of Seb.

There was a light breeze blowing, just enough to get the flag on top of the bridge moving but not enough to be unpleasant. They stopped numerous times to watch the ferries crisscross the harbour and the tiny yachts dart across the water. By the time they descended onto Cumberland Street in The Rocks Luci was famished. The combination of sex and walking had certainly fired her appetite. Seb ordered a big breakfast—bacon, eggs, tomato, spinach, mushrooms, hash browns. Luci had smashed avocado on toast with bacon on the side. She needed an energy boost.

'Can I ask you something?' she said as she cut into her bacon.

'Sure.'

'Why don't you have a girlfriend?'

'You mean, what's wrong with me that you haven't noticed yet?'

'No. Maybe.' Seb was teasing her but she was serious. 'Why *is* a guy like you single?'

'A guy like me? What *am* I like, exactly?'

'Oh, no, don't go fishing for compliments. Just answer the question.'

'Well, as long as you were thinking complimentary things, I'll explain,' he said. 'I want the freedom to do the things I want to do, to go where I want to go. Last year I spent about forty weeks in the country in four different towns. I don't see the point in long-distance relationships. I don't have a girlfriend because I don't want a serious relationship.'

'Have you *never* had a serious relationship?'

'Only one but that ended three years ago and I'm used to doing things my way now. I can't really see the need to commit to one person, not when so many relationships end badly.' He speared a mushroom with his fork before he looked up at her. 'Would you go through it all again?'

Luci nodded. 'I would. I liked being married,' she said honestly. 'I didn't like how my marriage *ended* but I'm not going to let that dictate how I spend the rest of my life. I liked being part of a couple, sharing my life.' It would be a long, lonely existence if she vowed never to go down that path again and if she was going to achieve her dream of motherhood she needed to be in a committed relationship. It wouldn't work any other way. Not for her at least, who had always dreamed of the whole package. 'You don't want that? Someone to share your life with? A family of your own?'

'No.' Seb drained the last of his coffee and pushed his chair back. 'I don't,' he said as he stood up.

Clearly that conversation was over. Luci would remember not to raise that topic again. She didn't want to rock the boat. There was no need to. They didn't need to have in-depth, detailed discussions about their hopes and dreams. This was all temporary, she reminded herself. It was supposed to be just a bit of fun.

They spent the next hour wandering through the markets in The Rocks before Seb took her to climb the south pylon of the bridge on their way back across the harbour. Their conversation stayed neutral, away from anything that could be considered remotely emotional, but Luci wasn't going to let it ruin her day. There was no rule that said he had to open up to her, and besides that he was the ideal date. He was attentive, funny, thoughtful and gorgeous. It had been a perfect first date.

Over the next ten days Seb took her on several dates that were almost as good. They visited the zoo and shopped in Paddington. They ate dinner in Chinatown, oysters beside the Opera House, burgers in Manly and fish and chips in Watson's Bay. But her favourite date was the day they'd hired a kayak and paddled to Store Beach. Just thinking about it now made her smile. She had been surprised by how many secluded coves there were around the harbour and she loved being able to escape the city so easily.

Store Beach was only accessible by boat, which meant it was quiet. She preferred the quieter beaches to the bustle of Bondi and Manly. Perhaps it was the country girl in her or perhaps it had something to do with the fact that when they had a beach to themselves they took advantage of that. They had made love in the water that day, something she was positive they wouldn't have been able to do at Bondi, and she knew she was going to file these memories away and revisit them when Seb was gone from her life. This might be temporary but she would always have the memories.

Spending time with Seb was therapeutic, mentally as well as physically. She felt happier than she had in a long time and she no longer thought about babies and failed marriages or Ben and his new wife, Catriona, every day. She had other things on her mind. She was becoming the person for the next stage of her life and she was starting to feel that she would be okay. She still wasn't sure that she'd be okay on her own but Seb was showing her how to put herself out there again. She knew that if she had been able to do it with him she'd be able to do it with the next guy. And maybe the next guy would be the one.

Her life was far from over. She would take her second chance. She would achieve her dreams, one way or another. Seb was right, she had time on her side and she wasn't going to let Ben take it all away from her. She would go after her dream and she would make it happen. She would learn as much as she could about herself while Seb was giving her that chance so she could grow and move forward.

Luci's time in Sydney was almost half-gone. The time was flying past; her days were busy and so were her nights. She wasn't sure how she was going to manage back in Vickers Hill. She couldn't remember how she used to fill her days. Work, housework, dinner with her parents and a game of netball once a week didn't seem like much now compared to what she was packing into her days in Sydney. So she'd better make the most of it.

She was feeling more confident and comfortable at work. She'd decided not to be so precious about comments and questions from clients as to whether or not she had children. They didn't know her circumstances so she replied with, 'Not yet,' and left it at that. She wasn't wearing a wedding ring so at least she was spared from those expectations that she and Ben had had. From the moment they'd got married that had been the next question. She'd initially used the excuses of 'We've only just got married' or 'We're saving for a house' but the questions hadn't really bothered her until she'd been trying to fall pregnant. She had needed to develop a tougher skin.

Spending time with Seb was definitely helping. He kept her mind and body busy and she no longer thought about having kids every hour of every day. She had relaxed. She had a little over four weeks remaining and she was determined to enjoy every second. The rest of her life could start after that. She had time.

But she very quickly got used to spending her days and nights with Seb and when he told her he needed to go away for a few days for work she found the prospect of being alone again quite daunting.

'I have been asked to go to Budgee to work in their community health clinic for a few days later this week. The doctor's wife and daughter have been injured in a car accident and the doctor has flown down to Sydney to be with them. There's no hospital there any more so there's no other cover.'

'Why have they asked you?'

He shrugged. 'I was there about eighteen months ago for six weeks so they figure I'll be more familiar with the work than others. And, besides, it's what I do.'

She knew that. He'd told her he spent a lot of time travelling to different parts of country New South Wales.

'You could come with me if you like.'

'How do you figure that?'

'The doctor's wife is a nurse so with her out of

action the town has lost their nurse and doctor. I could arrange a few days there for you as part of your course.'

Luci didn't care if people accused Seb of favouritism. Going with him was preferable to being left alone in Sydney, even if it was only for three days, which was how she found herself being driven down the main street of Budgee two days later.

It was a pretty town three hours west of Sydney over the Blue Mountains, with a small-town feel. The main street was wide, not dissimilar to main streets in most country towns across Australia, and this one was planted with oak trees and lined with beautiful old public buildings. A wide, grassy strip ran down the centre of the road. A military memorial stood at one end near the pub; a majestic building with wraparound balconies and elaborate wrought-iron railings. The two-storey red-brick post office stood in the middle of town opposite the limestone town hall. Further down the street, past the police station, the Catholic church faced off across the road from the Presbyterian one, standing sentinel at the end of town.

They had left Sydney early and arrived at the clinic by ten. They were going to spend the morning working there before visiting an aboriginal settlement in the afternoon.

'Budgee used to have a small hospital,' Seb explained as he turned off the main street, 'but the services gradually dwindled as the community decreased in size and as the roads and transport improved, making it unnecessary for each country town to have its own facilities. The government "consolidated"—their word—the services, which was all well and good in most cases except for emergencies. Budgee lost its hospital but retained a community health centre, which was moved into the old hospital ironically, and the local doctor spends two days a week here and three days a week in surrounding towns.'

Seb pulled into the car park of the old hospital and Luci followed him inside. She spent what was left of the morning doing health checks, just like she would have done in Sydney, along with fielding the same personal questions interspersed with questions about the health of the local nurse and her daughter.

For lunch she and Seb grabbed a meat pie from the local bakery and ate in the car as Seb drove them to the aboriginal settlement thirty minutes out of town. Budgee was in the centre of a wine-growing region and the town was surrounded by vineyards. It reminded Luci of Vickers Hill, having the same look and feel of home. Did Vickers Hill still feel like home? She wasn't sure. She'd changed since she'd been in Sydney. She was different now and she wasn't sure if she would be able to settle back into her old life.

Was it living in a big city that had changed her or was it Seb?

She didn't know the answer to that either, although she suspected the latter.

As they drove through the countryside she almost felt as though they were on a date. Seb was dressed casually in an open-necked, short-sleeved shirt that showed off his muscular forearms. His long fingers were wrapped around the steering wheel. Last night they'd been caressing her breasts and bringing her to another orgasm, and she could still feel some tenderness between her thighs after another night of lovemaking, but it was definitely not an unpleasant sensation.

Seb was tapping his index finger and humming along in time to the song that was playing on the radio. She looked at his face, at his perfect profile as the scenery flashed past. They were still driving past rows and rows of vines, dense with green foliage, and she was tempted to tell him to pull over. She wondered if they had time for a quick make-out session in the car. She hadn't behaved like that for years but something about him made her feel like a teenager again, a reckless, rebellious teenager with only one thing on her mind.

He turned his head to look at her; he must have felt her scrutiny. He took one look at her expression and winked, and she knew he could tell what she was thinking.

She blushed and he laughed, rich and throaty, as he turned his attention back to the road.

'Hold that thought,' he said. 'There'll be time for fooling around later but we can't turn up at the settlement looking like we've just tumbled out of bed. Or out of the bushes.' He grinned and his eyes flicked briefly back to her.

A quick glance at her chest and Luci could feel the heat rising from her. The only thing stopping the windows from fogging up was the fact that it was almost as warm outside the car as inside.

If he looked at her like that once more she was going to have to pull on the handbrake and have her way with him.

'Pity,' she said as she reached across the console, ignoring the handbrake, and rested her hand at the very top of his thigh. She slid her hand between his thighs so her fingers rested against his groin. If he was going to make her sweat she was going to make sure he joined her. Two could play at that game. 'We could pull over and sneak down between the rows of grapes and make love on the ground between the vines.'

'You'll get covered in dirt.'

'I was planning to go on top,' she responded.

'Luci,' he groaned. 'That's not playing fair. I need to concentrate.'

'Are you sure we haven't got time for a quick stop?'

'Positive,' he said, removing her hand from his groin and putting it back in her lap. 'But we will have all night and I promise I'll make the wait worth your while,' he said as he drove past the signpost that welcomed them to the settlement of Frog Hollow.

She sighed and looked around as Seb drove down the main street. She needed to get her mind back on the job.

'So tell me again what I'll be doing here,' she said, trying to focus less on Seb and more on her duties.

'It does depend on who turns up but general health checks are the norm. BP, cholesterol tests, with referral for any high readings, plus counselling will take up most of your time. Just keep in mind there are different issues facing this population. Diabetes, eye disease, cardiovascular conditions, kidney disease and ear infections all tend to be more prevalent in the indigenous community and a lot of the problems arise because they don't have access to health care.'

'I remember what you told us when you gave the lecture.'

'Well, you're about to see it first-hand, although because the community of Frog Hollow made a decision to be a dry settlement we do see fewer issues here than elsewhere. There won't be scheduled appointments as such, we just see whoever turns up in whatever order they turn up, but expect to be busy as these remote clinics are only run once a month.'

Seb turned off the main street onto a side road that was made of dirt. Apparently only the main road in and out of town was tarred but the buildings were modern. Luci could see plenty of free-roaming chickens and dogs, as well as a number of kids riding bikes and playing in the street. There seem to be an awful lot of children not in school.

'There's no school in the settlement,' Seb explained, when Luci commented. 'The kids need to go into Budgee on the school bus but a lot don't make it in time. Today quite a few parents would have chosen not to send their kids to town because we were coming,' he said as he parked the car and switched off the engine.

Luci could see several people waiting, sitting on the veranda of the hall. She helped Seb to unload the medical kits from the car and take them into the hall. A temporary clinic had been set up at one end near the kitchen. There were two stations, one for her and one for him, basic and identical save for the fact that Seb's had an examination bed tucked against the wall, sectioned off behind a privacy screen.

They worked their way steadily through the locals who seemed quite content to sit and wait. They didn't seem impatient. They didn't seem to be watching the clock, like the clients in the city who always seemed to have somewhere else they needed to be. The pace suited Luci. It was nice to have time to stop and take a breath occasionally.

There were some things about home she hadn't missed—the lack of privacy, for example—but she hadn't realised just what a whirlwind life in Sydney was. The pace was frenetic, with everyone constantly on the go, but it wasn't until she had a chance to slow down that she realised how rushed she'd been.

From her station she could watch Seb working. He seemed to be primarily checking ears and eyes as frequently as she was checking blood pressures.

He looked up and smiled at her and she felt a warm glow suffuse her. They worked well together. They did other things well together too and she hugged that thought to herself. She was looking forward to the end of the day, looking forward to tonight.

She stripped off her gloves as she finished with her patient and went out to the veranda to call the next one, only to find there was no one else waiting. She wondered if their day was done, if they could return to Budgee and finish what she'd started.

She went back inside the hall and was preparing to pack away her things when she saw Seb incline his head at her and nod at his patient, and she knew he wanted her to join them.

Seb was looking into the ears of a little boy who looked about three or four years of age. The boy's mother sat beside him. She was heavily pregnant and the fabric of her summer dress strained across her belly.

'Nadine, this is Luci Dawson, one of the community health nurses,' Seb said as he switched sides to look into the little boy's left ear. 'Luci, would you mind checking Nadine's blood pressure for me while I finish up with Byron? This is Nadine's fifth pregnancy and she hasn't had any problems, but she hasn't had any antenatal care either and she's not sure of her dates. She thinks she might be about seven months but seeing as we're here I thought we'd do a bit of a check.'

'Sure.' Luci smiled at Nadine.

The woman looked much further along than seven months. Luci couldn't imagine not having any antenatal care herself but Seb had warned her that things were different out here. Nadine looked relaxed but Luci knew Seb was worried.

It was hard to pinpoint her age. Her brown skin was smooth and glowed but her eyes looked tired. She could be anywhere from twenty-five to thirty-five. Even so, a fifth pregnancy was a lot.

Luci wrapped the blood-pressure cuff around Nadine's arm and pumped it up. She popped the stethoscope in her ears and listened for the heartbeat followed by silence as the cuff deflated. Her blood pressure was fine.

'All normal,' she told Seb.

'Good.' Seb nodded. 'Byron seems to have another slight middle-ear infection, swimmer's ear most likely. I'll give him a course of antibiotics but no swimming for a week, okay? And before you go I'd like to listen to the baby's heart and take a couple of measurements, if that's all right. Can you just hop up on the bed behind the screen for me?'

Seb rifled through one of the medical bags and found the medication he wanted. He wrote Byron's name and the instructions on a label and attached it to the bottle.

Luci took the bottle and handed him the stethoscope. She picked Byron up and popped him on her hip and followed Seb around the screen. Protocol dictated that she needed to be present for the exam.

Nadine had already hoisted her dress up to expose her belly, which was as tight as a drum. Luci felt a familiar pull of longing and jealousy when she saw the woman's heavily pregnant frame but she tried her best to ignore it. She was a professional, she could do this.

Seb placed the bulb of the scope on Nadine's tummy and moved it around, listening for the baby's heartbeat. Luci watched him. She saw him frown and reposition the stethoscope. She could see Nadine hold her breath but then Seb smiled and Nadine relaxed and exhaled.

Seb pulled the stethoscope out of his ears and looped it around his neck. Luci handed him a tape measure, which he took but didn't immediately use.

'Well, that explains a few things,' he said as he smiled at Nadine. 'You're having twins.'

'Twins?' Nadine and Luci said in unison.

Seb nodded and his blue eyes sparkled. 'Now I know you've done all this before but this is the first set of twins you've had. I want you to have some antenatal care. I want you to make an appointment at the hospital in Dubbo—actually, I'll make it for you,' he said as he helped Nadine to sit up on the edge of the bed.

He pulled his mobile phone out of his pocket and scrolled through the address book, looking for the number. Nadine stood up and slipped her feet back into her flip-flops before taking Byron from Luci.

Seb had been put through to the right department and covered the speaker with his hand as he spoke to Nadine. 'Can you make it to Dubbo tomorrow afternoon?'

Nadine nodded and Seb confirmed the time.

'They will do an ultrasound scan,' he said as he ended the call. 'It's important that they try to confirm your dates and check that everything is on track. Any dramas, make sure you call the Budgee clinic. I'll still be there tomorrow and I'll phone Dubbo for an update,' he added, wanting to make sure that she understood he'd be around to keep an eye on her. He handed Nadine a card with the Budgee clinic number on it and added the number for the Dubbo hospital, along with the appointment time.

'Do you think she'll keep the appointment?' Luci asked as they hit the road a little later for the return trip to Budgee. Flocks of galahs and sulphur-crested cockatoos were feeding at the side of the road. The cockatoos rose up in a squawking mass as the car passed them but the little pink and grey galahs seemed oblivious. They kept their heads down, pecking away at the gumnut seeds that were strewn on the ground.

'I hope so. Twins are obviously trickier to deal with, and gestational diabetes is high in the indigenous population so I'd like her to have the proper care. It'll be another month before anyone is back out at Frog Hollow. Anything could happen in that time.'

Luci's muscles groaned in protest as she lowered herself onto a child-sized kindergarten chair.

Muscles she'd forgotten she had ached and every time she moved she was reminded of the night before. She'd been stretched, bent and contorted into all sorts of positions last night but she wasn't complaining even if her muscles were. She and Seb had barely made it back to the motel before tearing each other's clothes off. Their desire had been building all afternoon until it had reached fever pitch and they had almost sprinted to her room and spent the rest of the evening making love, stopping only briefly to shower and grab some food before they'd gone back to her room. Luci knew they must have looked like they had been having frenzied sex but she hadn't cared any more. It hadn't been like home. She could behave as she pleased out here and it pleased her to misbehave with Seb.

She smiled to herself as she thought about what they'd got up to, until she realised that the preschoolers sitting at the table with her weren't going to give her time to daydream.

She was spending the afternoon in the childcare centre and kindergarten attached to the community health clinic. The work was pretty much the same, assessing the development of the children, but the approach was different. Instead of a formal appointment, Luci played with the children in the kindergarten environment, doing surreptitious development checks. Sitting with the kids while they drew pictures or constructed masterpieces out of cardboard rolls, boxes, egg cartons and metres of sticky tape gave her a chance to assess their hearing, speech and fine motor skills. Later she'd play outside with them in the sandpit and on the climbing equipment, observing their balance, co-ordination and gross motor skills.

If she noticed any issues she could then make referrals to the visiting therapists but, again, making appointments didn't necessarily work. Appointment times were not generally considered fixed and Luci had been told that a lot of the time the health-care staff just had to hope that some of the kids were in attendance at playgroup when the visiting therapists were in town.

Luci was writing a child's name on the cardboard robot that he'd made when she noticed Nadine and Byron coming into the centre.

Nadine looked tired today, definitely not as fresh as yesterday. The circles under her eyes had darkened and Luci thought her face looked a little pinched and drawn, as if she was in pain. Luci stood up. 'Nadine, hello. Are you on your way to Dubbo?'

Nadine nodded. 'I thought I'd drop Byron here while I went for my appointment, if that's okay. He knows this kindy.'

Budgee was about halfway between Frog Hollow and Dubbo. Nadine had had to pass through town in order to reach Dubbo.

'Sure,' Luci replied as Byron ran off to play. 'Are you feeling all right?'

'I didn't sleep well and my back is a bit sore. I think I might have pulled a muscle when I picked Byron up this morning.'

'Have you got time for a cup of tea or water? Why don't you sit down and I'll get you something to drink?' Luci offered. But before she could usher her to a chair Nadine clutched her stomach and looked as if she was about to burst into tears.

'What is it?' Luci asked.

But Nadine didn't answer, she just looked down at the floor. Luci followed her gaze.

Nadine was standing in a pool of water.

CHAPTER SEVEN

'THAT'S NOT GOOD,' Nadine said.

Luci agreed but at least Nadine was in town, and Seb was only metres away in the building next door.

But before Luci had a chance to say anything further Nadine gasped and doubled over.

'Contraction?' Luci asked.

She looked up at Luci and her dark brown eyes were filled with fear. She nodded and said, 'It's too early.'

Luci knew that Nadine was unsure of her dates and today's appointment had been an opportunity to narrow them down, but there was the distinct possibility that it was far too early. In some cases labour could be delayed, even if the membranes had ruptured, but that was a clinical decision and once the contractions had started Luci knew there was very little they could do.

'Dr Hollingsworth is just next door,' Luci said, trying to sound calm and reassuring even as she fought back her own concerns. 'Do you think you can walk or shall I fetch a wheelchair?'

'I can walk if I can lean on you.'

Jenny, the child-care director, had seen what was happening and she came across the room, carrying an armful of old towels. Being a centre filled with preschoolers, they were well equipped for dealing with accidents similar to this.

'Jenny, we need to leave Byron here,' Luci said as Jenny dropped the towels on the floor.

'Of course.' She squatted down to mop up the mess. 'What about your older children?' she asked Nadine.

'They'll go home on the school bus,' Nadine managed to say, before another contraction swamped her. She gripped tightly onto Luci's arm. The contractions were close together and strong. Luci didn't like the look of this at all.

She needed to get Nadine next door to Seb. And quickly.

Byron was engrossed with a big box of building blocks and trucks and didn't look up as Luci ushered his mother out of the centre.

'Heather, can you call Seb, please?' Luci started speaking to the receptionist in the community health clinic as soon as she and Nadine walked through the clinic doors. 'And an ambulance. Nadine is in labour.'

Heather stood up from behind the desk. 'Take her through here,' she said, directing Luci into one of the old hospital rooms. She wheeled a trolley over to the bed and handed Luci a hospital gown. 'There are gloves, scissors and basic clinical supplies on here. I'll call Seb and the ambulance and then check back to see if there's anything else you need. We're not fully equipped any more but I'll do my best.'

Luci nodded her thanks. 'You'd better phone ahead to Dubbo and warn them too. Nadine was on her way there for an antenatal appointment,' she added as Heather left the room. She turned back to Nadine, who was still clinging to her arm. 'Let's get you into this gown so that Dr Hollingsworth can examine you when he gets here.'

'Can you stop the labour? It's too early.'

Luci shook her head. 'Once your waters have broken there's nothing much we can do. These babies are on their way.' The best they could hope for was that the ambulance arrived before the babies did.

Seb hurried in just as Luci had finished helping Nadine to change.

'Nadine! I wasn't expecting to see you today. What's going on?' He sounded cool, calm and collected but there was no doubt he'd come at a run.

Luci handed him a paper hospital gown and he slipped his arms into the sleeves and waited as Luci tied the strings before he repeated the process for her. He washed his hands and pulled on a pair of surgical gloves as Luci wrapped a BP cuff around Nadine's arm.

'Let's see what's happening,' he said, as he positioned himself at the foot of the bed and got

Nadine to lie back and bend her knees. 'Eight centimetres dilated,' he said.

There wasn't going to be much time to spare. But just as Luci was praying that the ambulance was close by Heather came into the room and dashed her hopes.

'The ambulance is forty-five minutes out of town at the scene of a car accident. They'll get here as quickly as they can but expect them to be a while,' she informed them.

Nadine was in the middle of another contraction and Luci didn't think she'd heard a word Heather had said, which was probably just as well. It wasn't great news but it didn't appear to faze Seb.

'It looks like your babies are going to be born in Budgee,' Seb told Nadine once her contraction had passed. 'Luckily for you, we've done this before.' There wasn't a trace of panic in his voice and he even had Luci believing it would all be all right.

'You okay?' He looked at Luci and mouthed

the question. Nadine wouldn't be able to see his lips as her belly was blocking her view.

Luci wasn't sure. She didn't want to deal with a woman in labour. She'd managed to cope with Nadine's pregnancy yesterday, but actually delivering babies was a different thing altogether. But Seb didn't need to hear about her issues now. He needed her help. Somehow she'd get through this. She would focus on one thing at a time.

She nodded. Seb needed her. She would do her best to keep it together and wouldn't think about things that were out of her control.

'How quick were your other labours?' Seb asked Nadine. 'Have you been caught off guard before or have you been able to get to the hospital?'

'My third one was fast. She was born out at Frog Hollow.'

'But other than that it all went fine?'

Nadine nodded, unable to speak as another contraction gripped her. She was covered in a sheen of sweat and Luci wiped her forehead with a flannel.

'Were there any complications with your other deliveries?'

'No,' she puffed.

Seb picked a stethoscope up from the trolley and listened to the babies' heartbeats. They were both around one hundred and forty beats per minute—perfectly normal. Everyone else might be stressed but at least the babies weren't.

Heather returned and this time she was wheeling two small cots side by side. She parked these in the corner of the room and lifted out a pile of blankets and a set of scales. She wiped out the cots and folded some of the blankets, putting them back into the cots to act as makeshift mattresses before covering them with clean sheets. 'We had these in storage but there's not much else,' she said. 'There's pethidine if you need it but that's about it.'

Seb got the message. He doubted he had time for pethidine to work to provide any pain relief for Nadine—these babies were in a hurry and Heather's underlying message was that there was nothing else on hand to help him manage premature infants medically. There were no drugs, no Vitamin K injections, no heat lamps and no emergency team standing by.

Babies had been born for thousands of years without all the modern interference but Seb knew the survival rate of premature twins had been low in those days. He would do his best and hope that the ambulance arrived soon. He prayed silently that everything would go right.

His gaze swept the room, looking for anything at all that might come in handy. There was an oxygen tank attached to the wall. He looked at Luci and then back at the cylinder. 'Can you see if that works?' he asked her.

Luci put down the flannel and crossed the room. She had been very quiet and he hoped she was coping okay with the drama, he wasn't really sure how much experience she had with this sort of situation. But her movements were practised and efficient. She knew the basic procedures and he just had to hope that he could prevent an emergency.

Luci opened the valve on the oxygen tank. She nodded.

That was one thing he had up his sleeve if needed, he thought as he turned back to Nadine.

Her labour was progressing quickly. That wasn't surprising given that it was her fifth pregnancy and delivery, but Seb wished it wasn't so. He would much prefer it if she could hold on until the ambulance reached them but that was looking highly unlikely because he could see the first baby's head crowning.

'I want to push,' Nadine told him.

He'd barely had time to check the position of the babies but there was no going back now. 'Okay. We're ready to go.'

Nadine's knees were bent. Luci stood beside her, holding her hand.

'Push,' he instructed.

He reached between her thighs and eased the baby's head out.

'Okay, relax now. Wait for the next contraction.'

Nadine panted swiftly between contractions and with the following one Seb delivered the baby's shoulders. The little girl slid out swiftly and he hoped it was because Nadine's body was familiar with the process and not because the other baby had kicked it out. He didn't want to deal with a breech presentation as well as the premature delivery of twins.

'It's a girl,' he told Nadine. She came out yelling and Seb placed her on Nadine's chest. Luci had loosened the hospital gown at Nadine's neck so the baby could lie skin to skin on her mother but Seb couldn't leave her there for long. She needed to be checked and kept warm and he needed to get ready to deliver the second baby.

'Can you do the Apgar test?' he asked Luci as he cut the cord.

Luci nodded and reached for the baby. 'I'll just check her out,' she explained to Nadine. 'You've still got some work to do.'

Seb briefly watched Luci holding the baby. It suited her. She had an expression of contentment and he hoped for her sake that she had a child of her own one day. He knew that was what she wanted.

'One minute Apgar eight out of ten. Pulse ninety-six, tinge of blue in the fingers,' Luci said as she put the baby on the scales. He was aware of her weighing the baby as she updated him. 'Two point four kilograms,' she said as she wrapped the baby. There was no time to clean her up as she needed to be kept warm and Luci needed to be ready to help with the second delivery.

Nadine's contractions were continuing strongly. The second twin was on its way. He checked what was happening and breathed a sigh of relief when he felt Twin B moving down into the pelvis.

Seb had to rupture the membrane for Twin B and the next thing he saw was the baby's head crowning. Thank God it wasn't breech.

'Five-minute Apgar nine out of ten,' Luci said, updating him on Twin A. 'Colour is good, heart rate ninety-eight.'

He nodded in acknowledgement to Luci but spoke to Nadine. 'Okay, time for number two. You can push with the next contraction.'

The second twin was slightly bigger but was delivered just as easily. He handed the little boy to Nadine then checked the cord before clamping and cutting it. Nadine had a quick cuddle before Luci took him to assess.

'Six out of ten. Pulse ninety-four. Sluggish re-flexes, blue extremities, resp. rate thirty-five.'

The little boy was bigger, but not as healthy as his sister.

'He needs oxygen,' Luci said, and Seb knew she was looking to him to fix the problem. They had oxygen but how was he going to get it into a premature infant?

He looked around the room for inspiration as he prayed that the ambulance would hurry.

His gaze rested on the acrylic bassinettes.

'Can you connect some tubing to the oxygen cylinder?' he asked Luci as he covered Nadine with a blanket. The little boy was his priority now and there was nothing else he could do for Nadine until the ambulance arrived. If he could manage to hold the two bassinettes together he would be able to fashion a makeshift oxygen tent, which would be better than nothing in the short term. Taking the little boy from Lucy he placed him in a bassinette alongside his sister. He emptied the second bassinette and inverted it over the first. He grabbed a roll of medical tape and ran it around the edges of the cribs, taping them together. There was an opening where the sides had been cut down that would allow the carbon monoxide to escape. The 'tent' would be less efficient than he would like but it would be good enough.

Luci had connected the tubing to the oxygen cylinder. She passed the end to him and he slid it into the bassinette, taping it in place too.

'Run it at eight litres per minute,' he said as Heather came back into the room.

'The ambulance is five minutes away,' she told them, and Seb thought that was the best sentence he'd ever heard. He could handle five more minutes.

He left Luci to keep an eye on the babies as he spoke to Nadine. 'Your babies are okay. Your daughter is doing well, your little boy is having a little bit of difficulty breathing so we need to give him some oxygen, but the ambulance is almost here and will transfer them to Dubbo hospital.'

'What about me?'

'You'll go too.'

'Byron?'

'I've put him on the school bus with your other kids,' Heather said as she returned to the room with the ambulance officers in tow. 'Will there be someone home in Frog Hollow to take care of them?'

Nadine nodded. 'My husband is there and my sister will give him a hand.'

The next fifteen minutes passed in a flurry of activity as the ambos stabilised the babies and Seb gave Nadine an oxytocin injection and de-livered the placentas.

Somehow they got the whole family into the back of the ambulance and Seb breathed a sigh of relief as he closed the back doors and watched the ambulance take off.

When he went back into the community health clinic Heather was rescheduling the rest of the day's appointments. She was proving to be worth her weight in gold today.

He left her to it and went to help Luci tidy up the makeshift delivery suite.

She was stripping the bed and had her back to him but he saw her lift her arm and wipe her hand across her face and he realised she was crying. Were they happy or sad tears? Her shoulders were shaking and as he got closer he could hear her sobs. It sounded like her heart was breaking.

He put a hand on her shoulder. 'Luci, what's the matter?'

She turned around but she was crying so hard she couldn't talk. He wrapped her in his arms and held her tightly until her tears eased but didn't stop completely. He brushed her hair from her forehead and kissed her gently. 'What is it, Luce? Tell me what's wrong.'

'I can't do this any more,' she sobbed.

'Can't do what?'

'Deliver babies. It's one of the reasons 1 left Vickers Hill, seeing other women holding their newborn babies. I can't do it.'

He frowned. 'You'll get your turn,' he told her. 'We've talked about this.'

But Luci was shaking her head. 'You don't understand.'

'Explain it to me, then.'

'Not here. I need to go home.'

'Home?' he asked. 'To Vickers Hill?'

She shook her head and gulped air as she tried to get her emotions under control. 'No. Back to the motel.'

He was happy to call it quits. It was almost the end of the day and hopefully Heather had managed to reschedule the remaining appointments. Rarely was anything so urgent with community health that it couldn't be pushed back. He would start earlier tomorrow if necessary, before they headed back to Sydney. Right now Luci was his priority.

He had bundled her into the car and driven her back to the motel and now she was sitting on the edge of the bed. Her face was blotchy and her eyes were red but she had stopped crying. He boiled the kettle to make tea, wondering if he should call room service for something stronger, but decided to wait.

He handed her a cup of green tea. 'What's going on?' he asked.

'I don't like delivering babies.'

He frowned. 'What's not to like? I agree, sometimes things can get a bit difficult but we had a really good outcome today, all things considered.'

'I know and I'm happy for Nadine but I find it soul destroying. It just reminds me that the thing I want most in my life isn't a possibility.'

'What are you talking about? We've had this conversation…you're young, you've got time.'

'It's not time I need,' she said with a shake of her head. 'There are some things I love about small country towns and there are things I can live without. Like delivering babies. That's part of the reason I wanted to get out of there. I don't want to deliver other people's babies. Not when I can't have my own.'

'What do you mean?'

'I can't have kids.'

He wasn't sure if he was following the conversation properly. 'But you told me you and your ex-husband were planning on starting a family.'

'We were trying to get pregnant. It didn't happen.'

'But that doesn't mean you can't have them. It just means it hadn't happened yet.'

'We tried for eighteen months. Nothing.'

'It still doesn't mean the problem lies with you.'

'I'm pretty sure it does. Ben has remarried and is expecting a baby with his new wife.'

Wow. He hadn't seen that coming.

'Why haven't you told me this before?' he asked.

'Because it was irrelevant to you.'

He was momentarily affronted until he realised she was right. Their relationship had no strings attached.

But that didn't change the fact that Luci was upset and his natural instinct was to try to fix things. Although this could be a slight problem. He might be out of his depth.

'I guess it's not,' he agreed. 'You've spoken about wanting to have kids but you never mentioned you couldn't.' He was surprised at how hurt he felt that she hadn't confided in him but he wasn't stupid enough not to realise that he hadn't confided in her either. There was plenty of information he had kept to himself so why should he be upset to find she was no different? He didn't normally have double standards. 'Do you know what the problem is?'

Luci shook her head. 'No.'

'You haven't been tested?'

'It's a long story.'

'I'm not going anywhere.' Never had a truer word been spoken. They were in the middle of New South Wales. They had nowhere to go, nothing else to do. He had all the time in the world.

Luci sipped her tea. 'The doctors said the same thing as you did initially. They told us we were young and healthy and there was no reason to worry. They said we should try to relax, try to just enjoy it, and if, after a year, we weren't pregnant then they'd do tests. So we listened and decided to keep trying. I had no idea how hard it would be to "relax" in that situation. We kept working. We thought we'd pay off some more of our mortgage and Ben wanted to expand the family business and suddenly eighteen months had passed. So we went back to the doctor and tests were suggested.

'We started the process but by now we were worried. We started discussing what we would do if the tests showed a problem. Would we go down the IVF path? That's expensive and we weren't sure how we would afford it. We were already stressed and things just got worse, and then Ben met Catriona. When Ben left me there didn't seem any point in continuing the testing process and when I heard that Catriona was expecting a baby I figured I had my answer.' She shrugged. 'It didn't matter what the tests showed. The problem was with me.'

Seb could understand her devastation and her logic but that didn't mean she was right. 'But it could have been any number of things.'

'Well, until I find someone who I want to try again with it doesn't matter. What matters is trying to get on with my life. Ben took away my marriage and I've recovered from that, but he also took away my dream of having a family. Even if the problem lay with me as a couple we could have adopted or fostered kids, we could have made something work, but now I either have to give up on my dream or start again. I decided to start again. I will do it. I want this more than anything but it still hurts when I see pregnant women or women with their babies. It reminds me of what I might never have and it's part of the reason I wanted to move away from working in a country hospital. I had to assist with deliveries and I'd want to be happy for the parents but every time it just felt like my heart was breaking.'

'Working in family and community health might be just as difficult.'

'I know. I'm coming to realise that,' she sighed. 'But it's still an area that interests me. It's a double-edged sword in a way. I want to work with kids but I didn't think about the fact that so many women with young children would be pregnant with another one. But I'm hoping that eventually I'll feel better about it. It will either wreck me or help me but I don't expect it to happen overnight. One thing at a time.

'I've got over the end of my marriage, perhaps one day I'll accept that I can't have a family, but for the moment I just prefer not to talk about it. Not talking about it means I can try to ignore it. It's obvious the problem lies with me, but I'm not ready to think about what it means.'

All along Seb had had the feeling that she'd been running away and now he knew why. He couldn't blame her for not wanting to be around when her ex's new partner had the child she'd been longing for.

And now it was Seb's turn to feel as though his heart was breaking. In sympathy with Luci. *I'm so sorry.* What else could he say?

But he couldn't help her. There was nothing he could do. As much as he wanted to, he couldn't fix this. He couldn't give her what she wanted but he could take care of her. At least for now.

He lay on the bed with her and wrapped her in his arms and waited until she fell into an exhausted sleep.

But sleep eluded him. He lay in the dark and thought about Luci.

It had been a long time since anything, or anyone, had affected him this strongly. Since anyone had made his heart ache.

This was exactly what he'd been trying to avoid. He didn't want to feel. He didn't want to hurt for someone else. And he didn't want to think about what that meant.

In the space of three weeks he had seen her ecstatic, nervous, passionate, playful, flirty and full of despair. Unlike him, she wore her heart on her sleeve. He felt he had known her for much longer and he knew he would miss her when they parted ways, but their time was limited. He would be leaving Sydney in a little over a fortnight. This wasn't a long-term proposition and her problem was not his to solve. As much as he'd like to, he couldn't fix things for her and she hadn't asked him to.

He would enjoy the next few weeks, distract her and hopefully take her mind off her problems. He would give her time to heal and then he'd let her go.

* * *

Luci picked up her wine glass and followed Seb up the steps of his boat and around to the forward deck.

The carpenter had finished installing the new kitchen while she and Seb had been in Budgee. The boat was finished, still unnamed but finished, and to celebrate Seb had invited her to spend the weekend on board. Seb had cooked a simple meal of steak and salad, the new kitchen had been tested and the new bed christened. So far the weekend was fabulous.

The boat bobbed gently on the calm waters of the Hawkesbury River. It was a beautiful warm night. There were thick clouds on the horizon and rain had been forecast. The air was heavy with humidity but so far the rain held off. The sunset had been incredible and, for now, the sky was clear and black.

Luci sat beside Seb and he slipped his arm around her shoulders, tucking her in against him. She was naked under her cotton dress and Seb wore only a pair of shorts. His body heat radiated out to her. She leaned back against the windshield of the boat and looked up at the sky. It was sprinkled with tiny stars that looked like diamonds on black velvet.

There were no other lights, on the water or on the shore. She felt like they had the world to themselves. Luci sighed. Seb was constantly surprising her with their dates and this one was particularly romantic. Lying on the deck of the boat, feeling like they were the only two people in existence, she could see the attraction of having somewhere to escape to. It was quite possibly a necessity in order to maintain your sanity if you lived in a city like Sydney, but she still couldn't imagine making this her life. As romantic as the night was, she imagined it would be a very isolated existence with no one to share it with.

'Do you think you'll ever get lonely out here on your own?'

'Maybe,' Seb replied. 'But that's a chance I'm willing to take. I've never been lonely before.'

'You've never had anyone else stay?'

He shook his head. 'No.'

'Why is that?' Luci was curious and also flattered to think she was the first, but realised there could just as easily be another explanation that had nothing to do with her. 'Was it because the boat wasn't ready?'

'No. I've stayed the night many times but I've never felt the need to share this with anyone else before.'

'Why did you ask me?'

'I thought you might like it,' he said simply.

'Not to keep you company?'

'I'm happy with my own company.'

That had been a question that had been bothering her since the first time she'd set foot on his boat. His desire to have an escape, to keep a bachelor pad of sorts had seemed at odds with someone who was so vital and charismatic.

'Have you never thought about sharing your life with someone?' She knew he'd had at least one lengthy relationship but she still wondered why it hadn't developed into something more serious. He was only thirty-one. Far too young to have decided to spend his life alone. What had happened that had made him so solitary?

Despite her divorce Luci hadn't given up on finding love again. She wasn't assuming Seb would want to share his life with her but she wondered what had happened to make him so against the idea of sharing his life with anyone.

'Once upon a time I assumed I would marry and have kids, that it was something that was in my future. But it was just that. In the future. I assumed it would happen one day but I had no real plans that it had to happen by a certain point in my life. I guess I thought I would finish my studies, get married, eventually have a couple of kids, but it hasn't turned out that way. And I'm okay with that. I'm okay on my own.'

She had shared so much of herself with him— her hopes and dreams, her failures and disappointments. She knew him intimately yet she still knew very little about what had made him into the man he was today.

What had shaped him? What had led him to the decisions he had made? What were his hopes and dreams? Surely no one really hoped to spend their life alone, did they? Something must have happened to bring him to that conclusion.

'Yet now you've decided that you don't want that future. What has happened that has made you think you'd be better off alone?'

'I lost someone unexpectedly.'

'Your girlfriend?'

She felt his answering nod.

'What happened?'

'She was killed in a hit-and-run accident.'

'Oh, Seb.' Luci felt awful now. She'd forced the admission out of him and perhaps it wasn't something he'd wanted to share. She didn't know what she could say to make things better but before she could say anything Seb continued.

'It happened right outside our house. It was the day we were moving in together. Emma had parked opposite the house and she was carrying boxes inside. A car came round the corner and ran her over. I don't know whether she couldn't see where she was going, she might have stepped into the path of the car, but she hit her head when she fell. I guess she didn't have time to put her arms out. When I got home there was an ambulance in the middle of the street but it was too late. *I* was too late.

'She died from head injuries. I like to think she never knew what had happened but I don't think that's true. She didn't die instantly. It messed me up for a long time. Thinking about what she went through. How she suffered. And I don't want to experience anything like that again. That's why I've chosen to live my life the way I am.'

Finally Luci was able to understand. She couldn't imagine going through that experience. The trauma, the guilt, the despair. She knew he would have felt all those things, especially guilt. He would blame himself for not getting there sooner, not being there to help his girlfriend with the boxes. He would think he could have made the difference. Luci knew him well enough to know that he would struggle to forgive himself. She finally understood.

'Did they ever find the driver of the car?' she asked.

'No.'

He'd lost everything that day. He'd thought losing Emma had been the worst thing that could happen but things had got worse from there, much worse. But Seb wasn't sure if Luci could handle hearing about what had happened next. He lapsed into silence as he fought his demons. Fought with the guilt that still haunted him. He had never forgiven himself for not being there earlier. He had been held up at work, agreeing to see an extra patient. If he hadn't he would have been there. *He* would have been carrying those boxes and he wouldn't have lost everything.

'Seb?' Luci interrupted his thoughts.

Maybe if he explained everything to her she would understand why he was so different from her. Why he was the darkness and she was the light. Why he struggled to see the beauty in the world.

He continued. 'The coroner ordered a postmortem. The cause of death had to be officially determined in case Emma hadn't died from injuries sustained in the accident. They had to determine whether it had been natural causes or manslaughter. Not that it mattered in the end as the driver was never found,' he said, and he could hear the bitterness in his voice, 'but the post-mortem found that Emma was pregnant. I was going to be a father.'

CHAPTER EIGHT

HE FELT LUCI squeeze his hand in the darkness and heard her little intake of breath but she didn't speak, allowing him to continue.

'Emma had told her sister about the baby and apparently she was planning on telling me that night. She wanted it to be a surprise on what would have been our first night in the house. I've hated surprises ever since.'

He had lost everything. Not just his girlfriend but his future. He hadn't really ever thought seriously about being a father, he'd just assumed it would happen one day, but to be given that news and then have it taken away from him immediately had devastated him.

'Losing something I never had and never knew I wanted; I didn't understand how that could hurt so much.' It had destroyed his belief that good things could happen and he had only seen darkness for a long time after that. Mostly that was still all he saw.

'I imagine the feeling is similar to knowing that the thing you want most in the world is never going to happen for you.'

Luci's voice was thick with tears and he realised she did understand how he felt. She would have had the same feeling over and over again, every month, when she had been desperate to fall pregnant and it hadn't happened. Month after month. But she'd got through it.

Had his confession been hard on her?

'I didn't mean to upset you,' he told her. He'd wanted her to understand. He wasn't sure why but it seemed important that he share his past with her but he hadn't meant to upset her.

'I'm okay. I'm upset for you.'

'My whole life changed in the space of a few minutes. I took a new direction after that. I never moved into the house. I couldn't bring myself to do it. I sold the house and bought my motorbike and this boat instead. I couldn't settle, I was restless, I still am. That was my attempt at domestic-ity, at living a normal life, and it didn't turn out as I'd planned. I lost everything at once, things I didn't even know I had, and it took me a long time to feel like my life was back under control. I think it's enough now to be responsible just for my own life. I don't ever want to go through that pain again.'

Over the past three years he had slowly recov-ered from Emma's death but he hadn't forgotten how he'd felt and he wasn't sure that he wanted to put himself out there again for love. 'I don't want to put myself in that position again.' He didn't ever want to be vulnerable again. He had worked hard to get back on top of things and he didn't ever want to lose his way again. He was deter-mined to be the master of his own destiny but that made it very difficult to let someone else in.

He had moved on, to a degree, but he knew the events of that day had changed him and he never again wanted to feel that pain of loss that he felt was inevitable if he opened up his heart. So he had lived a solitary existence.

He didn't want to have a home. He didn't want to put down roots. Becoming invested in something, attached to something, scared him. He knew how easily it could be ripped away. 'When you love someone it isn't for ever. It can't be. Life doesn't work like that.'

'No one is meant to live a whole lifetime alone,' Luci argued. 'There are highs and lows, disappointments and tragedies, as well as happiness and joy in life, and *I* think it's better to share those times with someone else. Sharing those feelings can soften the lows and enhance the highs. Joy and sadness are both better shared. Let me show you.'

She stood on the deck and lifted her dress over her head. She wore nothing underneath the thin cotton shift. She stood before him, naked and gorgeous, and offered him solace.

His reaction was immediate. He knew how the pleasures of the flesh could wipe out the traumas of the past, even if only temporarily. He'd had plenty of experience in that method of recovery over the past three years but never had he felt the satisfaction that he felt when he was with Luci. He got a sense of peacefulness with her and that was something that had never lasted before. Along with the physical release Luci was somehow able to provide emotional release too.

He pushed his shorts down and over his feet so he too was naked and knelt before her. His erection stood to attention, stiff and strong, but he ignored it.

He ran his hands up the insides of her thighs, parting them.

She opened her legs wider for him as his fingers reached the junction of her thighs. He slid his fingers inside her. She was warm and moist.

She moaned and pushed against him as he ran his thumb over the bud at her core. He replaced his thumb with his tongue and all his troubles were forgotten as he licked and sucked until she shivered with his touch. He cupped her buttocks with his hands and held her against him, burying himself in her, losing himself in the sweet saltiness of her.

She gasped and held his head with her hands.

She moaned again, a little louder. Spread her legs a little wider. Let him in a little deeper.

He felt her legs start to shake. He rose and lifted her off her feet and she wrapped her legs around him. He was vaguely aware of thunder rumbling in the distance as he turned and pushed her against the windshield. The storm was on its way.

He locked her between his body and the slope of the glass. Bent his head and licked her breasts as he drove himself deep inside her.

Her skin glowed ghostly pale in the moonlight and he could see the four freckles, dark against her skin, on the swell of her breast. Over her right shoulder he could see the Southern Cross, the diamonds in the sky that would always remind him of her.

He ignored the storm and the stars and the memories as he focused on feeling, touching and tasting. He rode the waves of pleasure with Luci.

He didn't miss Emma any more. He hadn't missed her for a long time. He'd taught himself to be alone but as he lost himself in Luci he realised all the other things he'd been missing. All the things that not feeling had deprived him of. The pleasure of sharing not just physically but emotionally.

He had shut himself off and Luci was helping him to open up again. She saw the good in the world. The brightness and the light. He had blocked that all out. Not wanting to risk being hurt, he had shut out all the beauty as well.

Her arms were around his neck and he felt her legs tighten around his waist as she met his thrusts, urging him to go faster. She was warm and wet as she clung to him. She was brightness and light. Even after what she'd been through she hadn't given up on the idea of love.

'Now, Seb. Now!'

She arched her back as she came, trembling in his arms.

He shuddered with the release as a fork of lightning split the sky, followed by a clap of thunder booming overhead just as they came together, sharing the pleasure.

He could smell her. She was warm and sweet.

He pressed his lips against her shoulder as he tasted her. She was salty and sweet.

Clouds drifted overhead, obscuring the stars, and he smelt the rain just before it began to fall. Fat, warm drops fell on their bare skin.

Luci was still in his arms and he carried her downstairs to his bed, their clothes abandoned on the deck as the storm raged overhead.

It passed quickly but he didn't notice. They lay in peaceful, contented silence. He wasn't thinking about love and loss. He wasn't thinking about anything other than the satisfaction and pleasure of having someone to hold.

Perhaps Luci was right. Maybe having someone to share things with could sometimes make things better.

He fell asleep with Luci in his arms as the storm rolled to the east.

Luci stowed her suitcase in the luggage compartment under the bus that was going to take her back to Vickers Hill. She climbed on board with mixed emotions. Her uncle had died three days ago so the trip home was tinged with sadness but while she was looking forward to seeing her family she wasn't sure if she was quite ready to be back in Vickers Hill. She didn't feel as if she'd been gone long enough to erase people's perceptions of her. Would they still think of her as 'poor Luci', the girl who couldn't keep her husband? Or would they have moved on to something else?

She was also wary about seeing Ben but she knew there would be no avoiding it. Her uncle had been married to his great-aunt. There weren't enough degrees of separation in country towns. She would have to see both Ben and his new wife, Catriona, and just to complicate things further Luci knew Catriona would be heavily pregnant. She was due to give birth any day now.

She could use Seb's cool head and rational thinking but he was hundreds of miles away. She knew he'd been worried about how she was going to cope with all the different stresses but she'd assured him she'd be fine. She didn't want him to worry, even though she was worried herself. She was a big girl. She'd have to cope. She couldn't expect Seb to fight her battles, he wouldn't always be there for her, but she admitted to herself it would have been nice.

Despite the fact that it had only been a few hours since he had dropped her at Sydney airport to catch the flight to Adelaide she was missing him already. But she was only planning on being gone for two days. She could last that long.

She had got used to his company very quickly. He made her laugh. He listened when she talked. He made her feel happy and positive. Plus he was gorgeous and smart and good in bed. What wasn't to like?

The only problem was that he didn't want to settle down.

So ultimately he wasn't the man for her. She knew that but it didn't stop her from wishing things were different.

She wanted to find the person she was supposed to spend the rest of her life with. There must be someone out there for her. It wasn't Ben and it wasn't Seb, not unless she could change his mind—an unlikely event—and she was running out of time.

She'd known from the very beginning that his time in Sydney was limited, as was hers, but his holidays started in eight days and she knew he was planning on leaving then. He was heading off on his boat, leaving her to finish her stint in Sydney. She would have another fortnight in Sydney on her own after Seb left and she was already dreading it, not looking forward to being on her own again. She wasn't looking forward to being without Seb, but there wasn't anything she could do about it.

Things were out of her control. She couldn't control his plans and she couldn't conjure up a man. She would just have to be patient.

At least she knew now that she could open her heart. Finding love shouldn't be impossible if she was open to it.

She closed her eyes and rested her head on the window as the bus chugged through the northern suburbs of the city. She fell asleep dreaming of

Seb and woke as the bus slowed on its approach into Vickers Hill.

She'd forgotten how dry and brown the countryside could get, even when it was only the beginning of summer. In five weeks she'd already grown used to being surrounded by water, by the ocean, and the blue and sometimes rainy grey of Sydney was very different from the brown and pale, washed-out grey of the Clare Valley.

The scenery was unfamiliar but the smell was the same. She could smell the dust in the air. It smelt like home but did it feel like home? She wouldn't know until she got off the bus.

The bus pulled up in the main street of Vickers Hill. She wanted to go and see Flick, there was so much to tell her, but she needed to see her parents first. She checked her watch. They would be having lunch. Her father would have taken the day off to bury his brother, Callum would have him covered, but even when he was working her parents had a tradition where her father would break for lunch and go home and eat with her mother.

Luci would join them and then attend the funeral. There would be time to see Flick later.

The funeral had gone as well as could be expected. A death was always sad but her uncle had been old and it had been his time. Luci couldn't help thinking that her father might be next, though. She would feel so differently if it had been her father's funeral. He was younger than his brother, but not by many years, and she wanted him to live long enough to see his grandchildren. She wanted to give him that gift. Her parents had nieces and nephews and great-nieces and great-nephews but Luci knew it wasn't the same thing as grandchildren.

Ben along with several of Luci's cousins and nephews had been the pallbearers for her uncle's coffin. She had watched Ben as he had helped to carry her uncle out of the church and into the graveyard beside it. Her parents supported her uncle's wife, her aunt by marriage and Ben's great-aunt, as they buried her husband.

Luci chatted to her cousins as everyone made

their way from the church to the wake, which was being held in the beer garden at the back of the local pub. She spent the next half-hour talking to familiar faces but she felt out of place. Having changed in the past few weeks, she wasn't sure she belonged here any more.

She was thinking about leaving, about excusing herself to get some breathing space, when she saw Ben approaching. She looked for Catriona but couldn't see her. She hadn't noticed her in the church either. It was too late to escape now as he was heading right for her, so she waited; she couldn't avoid him for ever.

He greeted her with a kiss and Luci waited to see what effect that had but she felt nothing. No regret. No desire. It was like greeting an old friend and she supposed that's now what they were. They had been friends for too long to cut him out of her life altogether. She could do platonic kisses.

'Hi, Luce, you're looking well.'

In contrast, she thought he looked tired. He was a little greyer at the temples. Perhaps a little bit heavier. It had only been a few months since she'd last seen him so how much could he have changed? Or was she just comparing him to Seb?

She pushed Seb out of her mind.

'Hello, Ben. How are you? How's Catriona? *Where's* Catriona?' Luci wondered if Catriona was too pregnant, too uncomfortable to stand at the funeral.

'She's in hospital. Our baby was born yesterday.'

'Oh.' Luci was taken by surprise. Why hadn't her mother told her? Warned her? Was everyone still trying to protect her?

Or perhaps with everything else going on in her family this week it had slipped her parents' minds. Her mother had a habit of telling her things twice or not at all, getting confused between what she'd told Luci's father and what she'd told Luci. Luci supposed she couldn't blame her for forgetting in the scheme of things. Ben and Catriona's baby didn't really matter to Luci, and why should it matter to her mother?

She didn't need protecting. She was sad for herself, but she didn't begrudge Ben his happiness.

She really had moved on, she realised. She'd been talking the talk but without really knowing. This was the test and it was good to find she could be happy for Ben.

'Congratulations,' she said.

Ben was watching her closely. 'I'm sorry. I didn't realise you didn't know. I thought someone would have said something. I wasn't planning on being the one to tell you.'

'It's okay. I would have found out sooner or later. What did you have?'

'A daughter.'

A baby girl. 'Details?' she asked, pleased to know she could remember the niceties.

'Seven pounds three ounces and we've named her Mia.'

Luci breathed a silent sigh of relief. She'd been worried that Ben might choose one of the names they had picked out and she was glad he hadn't. It was highly unlikely that she would get to use the names she'd chosen, Eve for a girl or Joe for a boy, but even so she didn't want Ben to use 'their' names.

'I'm happy for you,' she told him truthfully. She knew he wanted children just as much as she did. She couldn't begrudge him that happiness, but it didn't negate the sadness she felt that she was still childless.

She should go and find Ben's parents, her ex-in-laws, and congratulate them. She knew that by doing that, it would help to stop any unwanted smalltown gossip. She would be doing herself a favour. And it would give her a reason to say goodbye to Ben. She was ready for that. She didn't want him back but she couldn't deny that she was jealous of his new life. He had every-thing she wanted.

She excused herself and was relieved to see Flick making her way through the pub and into the garden. Luci forgot about seeking out her ex-in-laws and made a beeline for her friend, wrap-ping her in a big hug.

'God, it's so good to see you,' she said.

'Sorry I couldn't come to the funeral,' Flick replied as she hugged her back. 'Callum was covering the clinic for your dad so he needed me to help him.'

Flick had a sparkle in her eye. She looked well. Happy. But Luci was too preoccupied to pay any more attention than that.

'Why didn't you tell me Ben and Catriona had the baby?'

Flick shrugged. 'She was only born yesterday. I figured your mum would tell you and we'd talk about it today. Who did tell you?'

'Ben.'

'Oh, hell. Are you okay?'

Luci nodded. 'I think so. Sad for me, if I'm honest, but otherwise okay. I'll hold it together. I'm not going to give anyone here the satisfaction of seeing me fall apart. I'm tired of being the one everyone talks about.'

'Well, don't get your hopes up.' Flick laughed. 'No doubt they'll be talking about you again now that you're back and everyone has seen you talking to Ben.'

'I'm not back for good,' Luci responded, and

wondered whether that was really how she felt. Could she come back permanently?

She wasn't sure.

But where else would she go?

She had no idea.

'You're not thinking of staying in Sydney, are you?' Flick asked. 'Are you enjoying it that much?'

Luci kept quiet, which was a mistake.

Flick jumped straight to a conclusion. 'OMG, is it Seb?'

She'd told Flick a little bit about him. Not everything. She wanted to keep some of what they'd shared to herself but it had been obvious in her conversations that they'd been spending a lot of time together and Luci hadn't been able to keep the happiness from spilling into her voice.

'I'd stay in a heartbeat if he asked me to but I can't see that happening.'

When Luci saw the expression on Flick's face—eyes wide open, jaw dropping—she realised she'd said the words out loud and remembered that Flick was working with Seb's brother.

'Promise me you won't say anything to Callum!' she hissed.

'Why would I? But does Seb know how you feel?'

Luci shook her head. 'Of course not. It's just a bit of fun.'

'Seriously? That doesn't sound like you.'

'What do you mean by that?'

'Well, you have to admit that even for around here you settled down early. You were always the one who was going to have the serious relationships.'

'Seb is only in Sydney for another week. I can't afford to get serious.'

'So you're just using him for sex.'

'Shh!'

'Well, you are doing the deed, aren't you?'

'Yes.' Luci blushed, thinking about the sex. Where and when and how good it had been. 'And often,' she added, wanting to see Flick's reaction.

Flick laughed. 'You go, girl! So why is it just a bit of fun? Why can't it be more serious than that? It doesn't matter if he's leaving Sydney. You could go with him.'

'No.' Luci shook her head again, knowing she was trying to convince herself as much as Flick. 'It's not a long-term proposition. Not at all. We want different things out of life. He's great but he doesn't want to settle down. I can't afford to waste time on someone who doesn't want the same things as me.'

It was a pity. Such a pity. Luci understood why he felt that way but it was still a shame. He didn't know what he was missing.

But did she? Why was it that she was so desperate to have kids? Could she be content without them?

She didn't know what she was missing either but she just knew that something was. There was a yearning in her heart. Not only for a partner but for a family. She knew what she needed to make herself complete. A man wouldn't be enough. And if she knew that she needed to be a mother without ever having been one, who was to say that Seb couldn't know he didn't want to be a father? That wasn't for her to judge.

Flick opened her mouth and Luci had the suspicion that she was about to tell her something important but right at that moment the crowd went silent. All at once.

Heads turned as the noise ceased and all eyes were focused on the door that led from the pub out to the garden.

Standing in the doorway was Seb.

CHAPTER NINE

IT WAS IMMEDIATELY obvious that he wasn't from around here and it had nothing to do with the fact that he was a tall, dark, handsome stranger. You could always expect a few strangers at a funeral but Seb wasn't wearing the country uniform. All the male mourners were wearing smart jeans, their polished boots and a shirt that was obviously kept for best. Seb was wearing neatly ironed chino pants, a black T-shirt and his leather jacket. The other men all had suntanned faces with white foreheads where their hats sat, and despite the hours Seb spent on the water he didn't have the same weathered look of years spent outdoors.

The stunned silence was followed by a swell of murmuring as everyone tried to figure out who this man was. Luci could hear people asking each other if they knew him.

'OMG, what is he doing here?' she muttered.

She could feel Flick looking from her back to Seb and back to her and she knew Flick's jaw had dropped open again.

'Is that him?'

Luci nodded. She couldn't speak.

'Holy...' Flick said under her breath. 'He looks like more than just a *bit* of fun. He looks like a whole *lot* of fun.'

'Shush,' Luci said, whacking Flick on the arm before making a beeline for Seb. She had to get him out of the pub. People had only just moved on from discussing her and Ben and she knew there was no way they'd be able to resist talking about her again now that they'd laid eyes on Seb and realised he was here for her.

Was he here for her? she wondered as she was halfway across the room. Maybe he was here to see Callum? Although that made no sense what-soever. She knew that the two brothers didn't

even talk that often, so why would he have travelled halfway across the country to see him?

He was grinning widely by the time she reached
his side. His blue eyes sparkled and to keep herself from jumping into his arms she grabbed his
elbow and pulled him back through the doorway,
out of the garden and into the pub. She would
have kept walking too, wanting to get him right
out of the building and into the street, away from
flapping ears and prying eyes, but Seb planted
his feet and once he did that she had about as
much chance of moving him as a mosquito had
in a cyclone.

'What are you doing here?'

They were in a short, narrow corridor between
the pub kitchen and the rest rooms and it was
only a matter of time before they were inter-
rupted, but Seb didn't seem to mind. He leaned
against the wall and pulled her into him. She
could see he was about to kiss her and she wasn't
going to let him do that. Not in front of her family and the rest of the town.

She put her hands on his chest, keeping them

separated by a few inches of air, but the gesture hardly afforded her any protection. His chest was firm and solid under her fingers and his thighs were strong and powerful against her legs. She could feel herself melting into him as her resistance weakened. She might as well have let him kiss her, the effect would have been the same.

'I thought you might be finding things difficult,' he said. 'I wanted to be here for you.'

She was touched that he had even thought that, let alone jumped on a plane and somehow made it to Vickers Hill just hours after she had. He was gorgeous. She couldn't believe he was standing in front of her, in her home town, looking at her with his blue eyes and ridiculously long, dark eyelashes. She'd been wishing he was here and somehow her wish had come true. She wasn't going to deny that it was good to see him.

'I love it that you're here,' she told him. And she did, except for the fact that the gossip mill was going to go into overdrive again, but that wasn't his fault. She couldn't expect him to understand how her home town worked. She'd just have to deal with the questions later. 'But my uncle was old so while a funeral is never the best situation it's okay. I think my dad is going to find it hard but I'm all right.'

'I wasn't thinking about your uncle. I was thinking that you would be seeing Ben and Catriona. I thought that would be hard on you. I wanted to be here to support you.'

'Oh.' He really was incredible. She couldn't believe he had come all this way for her. 'Catriona had the baby yesterday.'

'Did you know?'

Luci shook her head.

'How are you feeling?'

'Mixed emotions, if I'm totally honest. I'm actually pleased for Ben that he's found happiness and I'm not sorry that he's had a child, but I am sorry that it might not happen for me.' She didn't want Ben, there was no sense of longing, of wishing they were still a couple. The spark was well and truly extinguished, but she did want what he had.

'I'm here for you. Just tell me what you need me to do. Do you want to get out of here?' he asked.

She did. Desperately. She wanted Seb to take her away from all this. Now that he was here she knew he would be all she could think about. But he'd asked her what she needed, not what she wanted. And she needed to have dinner with her parents.

She shook her head. 'I'm supposed to be having dinner with my family.' She didn't want to introduce him to anyone, she wasn't ready for that. She didn't want to explain or start any rumours. It wasn't worth it when it would all be over in a week. These considerate gestures that Seb insisted on making—turning up here to offer support, walking with her across the harbour bridge, bringing her a cup of tea every morning in bed—not to mention being simply gorgeous, were going to make it hard to walk away, but there was no other option. That was the agreement they had made. She wasn't ready for the end yet. But it wasn't her choice.

'Why don't you do that, then, and I'll see if I

can catch up with Cal and meet you later. After dinner.'

He didn't push her for an invite. He seemed to know what she needed before she did. She wanted to go with him now but knowing he would be waiting for her at the end of the day was enough. She was glad he was here.

She nodded. 'Okay. Where are you staying?' she asked, hoping he wasn't staying at Callum's. That was her house. That would be weird.

'I booked a room at the hotel.'

She didn't need to hear any more. That was perfect.

'Room eleven,' he added with a wink and a grin, and Luci nearly gave in right then. She was sorely tempted to ditch the family dinner in favour of jumping into bed with Seb.

But instead she had to be content with grabbing a fistful of his shirt and pulling him towards her. She kissed him hard, not caring who saw them. She didn't care any more. He had come all this way for her and she didn't want to waste a minute of the time they had left together.

She'd be gone again tomorrow. Let them talk.

'I'll see you later,' she said as she pushed him out of the pub.

Luci sneaked into her parents' house just before sunrise, avoiding the fourth and ninth floorboards in the hall because she knew they creaked. She felt like a teenager again, even though she knew she shouldn't have to worry. After all, she'd been married and divorced, but old habits died hard.

She hoped they were asleep. She didn't want to explain where she'd been, what she'd been doing. She had spent the night in Seb's bed and after saying goodbye he'd headed off early in order to make it back to Adelaide in time for his return flight.

Luci climbed into her old bed but she couldn't sleep. Her mind was turning in circles.

She needed to start planning her next move. To work out how she was going to fulfil her dreams. Seb wasn't going to be a part of that. She knew he didn't want a proper relationship and she was determined to fulfil her dreams of motherhood one way or another. She assumed it would have to be through adoption and she wanted to find a partner who would support her in that. She couldn't afford to waste time on Seb. They had eight more days together and then it would be over. They would go back to their own lives. She couldn't focus on Seb, there were more important things for her to worry about.

The decisions were hers to make and hers alone.

Luci disembarked from the plane in Sydney and switched on her phone. As expected, there was a message from Seb asking her to text when she arrived safely, but there was also one from her GP, asking her to call back. Luci waited until she got back to the apartment to return the call.

'Could you come in for a chat?' her GP asked. 'There's something I need to discuss with you.'

Her GP was in the neighbouring town to Vickers Hill. Luci hadn't wanted to see anyone with ties to her dad's clinic so ever since she'd got her driver's licence she'd made the fifteen-minute drive along the highway.

'Actually, I can't,' she said. 'I'm in Sydney. Is there a problem? I'll be here for another three weeks.' Luci couldn't imagine what it was about. She was perfectly healthy and so was everyone else, as far as she knew.

'Can you talk now?'

'Yes,' she said, sitting on the couch.

'I received a letter today from the lab that did your fertility tests. The letter contains your test results. Apparently they were upgrading their computer system at the same time that you went for testing and some of the results were mistakenly filed as "sent" when they were actually pending. The lab has only just realised their mistake. I'm sorry, I never realised that these weren't forwarded to you. You haven't been in for an appointment.'

'It doesn't matter,' Luci replied. 'It turns out the results were irrelevant.'

'What do you mean?'

'It was obvious that the problem was with me. Ben had no trouble getting Catriona pregnant. The results don't matter, it's not like I'm in a situation to have a baby now. I'm divorced and single, I'm not trying to get pregnant any more.'

'I still think you should know the results. It's not quite as simple as you think. The tests indicated that the problem wasn't solely with you.'

'What does that mean? Ben's reproductive system seems to work fine.'

'The problem was with the two of you together.' Luci frowned as Veronica continued. 'Your body was producing antibodies against Ben's sperm. It's very uncommon and especially rare to see in women, but it meant that your body was having a kind of allergic reaction to the sperm. The antibodies attach to the sperm and impair motility, making it harder for the sperm to penetrate the cervical mucus and therefore fertilise the egg. IVF would have been a relatively simple procedure for you. In your situation there would have been a high chance of success for the two of you.'

'What?' Luci couldn't believe what she was hearing. 'We could have had children?' They could have had the family she'd dreamed of?

'With IVF assistance, almost certainly,' Veronica agreed.

'How?'

'The sperm would be injected directly into the harvested egg. If the sperm aren't swimming freely there would have been no opportunity for your body to attack. The antibodies wouldn't have had a chance to attach to the sperm. With IVF a viable embryo would have been created and it would then have been implanted.'

'So I can have kids?' Luci still wasn't absolutely sure that she was getting the right message. Was that what Veronica was telling her? She held her breath as she waited for the final confirmation.

'Yes. Either with the right partner or with IVF.'

Luci breathed out as tears welled in her eyes.

'It's rare for a woman to produce anti-sperm antibodies so it's quite likely that with a different partner you wouldn't have the same issues,' Veronica went on, but Luci was only half listening. She was still processing the idea that she could have children.

'But don't forget, this condition is very success-fully overcome with IVF assistance. Identifying this is a good thing.' Veronica was still speaking. 'You and Ben may have been incompatible but that doesn't mean all men will be. And there's more good news. Your eggs were healthy. You're young and fertile. You have time. It will happen for you, I'm sure of it.'

'Thank you.'

Tears spilled out of Luci's eyes and rolled down her cheeks as she ended the call. Mixed emo-tions engulfed her. The news was incredible but it was tinged with anger and regret. Just when she felt she had come to terms with the demise of her marriage to find out that Ben's betrayal had robbed her of her dream of motherhood was almost too much to bear. When she had thought she couldn't fall pregnant she'd been able to for-give him for leaving her. She had blamed herself as much as him. But now?

If he had stayed they could have worked this out. With IVF *she* could have been the one who had just had a baby. She could be a mother now.

She needed to think. She needed a walk to help focus her mind. She changed into a pair of shorts and her sneakers and headed for the beach.

As she walked she realised it was unlikely that her marriage would have survived regardless. They had broken up because of the stress of infertility but Ben had very quickly moved on. If she'd been unable to rely on him to stick by her through that situation she knew she wouldn't have been able to rely on him for anything else. Quite possibly he would have run for the hills the moment the going had got tough. Quite possibly she would have ended up divorced with a baby.

Would she want to be a single mother?

Yes.

If she could have a baby without a partner she knew she would take that opportunity. She had never imagined herself as a single mother but she knew that if that was her only option she wouldn't hesitate any more. She still wanted a baby more than anything.

More than she wanted Seb?

Yes. Her heart ached with longing and her

womb ached with emptiness. A baby was very much her priority.

She had fallen in love with Seb but planning a future with him had never been realistic and especially not now. He was her second ever boyfriend and she wasn't even sure she could call him that. They weren't thinking about the future and he didn't want commitment. He didn't want to settle down and she was pretty sure he wasn't going to want kids.

She would have to break up with him. It was her only option.

She wanted it all but if she couldn't have it all she was going to choose motherhood, or the possibility of it at least, and if her dream was to become a reality she needed to find the man who could help her to make that happen.

Which meant she needed to break up with Seb.

He was starting his holidays at the end of the week. He was heading off in his boat so their relationship wasn't going to last any longer than that anyway, no matter what she wished for, so the best thing to do would be to end it now. Quickly and swiftly. Waiting a couple more days wasn't going to make it any easier. She needed to move on to the rest of her life.

The decision was made. Now all she had to do was tell him.

Telling him would give him the chance to change his mind if he wanted to and she knew she was still hopeful that he would make that choice. Perhaps he would decide that she was worth it.

The sun was low in the sky as she returned to the apartment. Her phone buzzed in her pocket. She pulled it out and looked at the caller ID. Seb.

'Where are you? Is everything okay?'

He sounded worried but she didn't think she could put his mind at ease so she opted for a simple reply. 'I'm almost home. I'll see you in a minute.'

But Callum's apartment wasn't home. And Vickers Hill hadn't felt like home either.

Luci knew she wouldn't be going back to Vickers Hill. She'd felt like a fish out of water there.

Everyone was settled or, worse, if they weren't she had known them all her life and she knew she wasn't going to find the man she was looking for amongst them. She needed new faces. New places. She had no idea where she would go but she knew she wouldn't go back.

She would need to find somewhere that felt right.

Also, she needed a man, or his sperm at the very least, and a place to live. But one thing at a time. Her first priority was to speak to Seb. She needed to tell him her decision. There was no point delaying. She needed to get on with things. She was a girl with a mission.

The door to the apartment was open. Seb was waiting for her. He still looked worried. There was a little crease between his eyebrows and his blue eyes were dark with concern. But she almost didn't notice. It was a hot night and he was dressed only in a pair of shorts. Shirtless and bare-chested, she found it hard to notice anything else.

He looked incredible. She'd almost forgotten how gorgeous he was. She should ask him to put a shirt on, she wasn't going to be able to concentrate when he was semi-naked, but she resisted. Why deprive herself of her last chance to see him like this? She could use the memory.

He greeted her with a hug. God, that felt good. His arms were strong, his embrace warm, and Luci could have stayed there quite happily for the rest of her life.

'I've missed you,' he said as he let her go. 'Is anything wrong?' He ran a thumb under her eye and Luci's knees buckled slightly at his touch. 'Have you been crying?'

Her tears had dried long ago but she knew her eyes would still be puffy and red. She wiped a hand across them. 'Yes. But they were happy tears, I think.'

'You think? What's going on?'

'I need to sit down.'

Seb ushered her to the couch. 'Can I get you anything?'

She shook her head. 'No. But I need to talk

to you.' Luci launched into her news. She knew if she waited she'd chicken out. She was sorely tempted to spend one last night with Seb and tell him tomorrow but it wouldn't be any easier then. She needed to do this now. 'I had a phone call from my GP today. She was calling about some test results. Results that I should have got ages ago but the lab made a mistake. I didn't really notice that the results hadn't come back because of everything else that was going on at the time between Ben and me.'

'Are you okay?'

'Yes. I'm perfectly okay. That was what she was ringing me about. Apparently I am perfectly healthy and fertile. I can have children. The problem wasn't with me. It was with *Ben* and me. But even so we could have had a family together if we'd stuck it out. IVF would have fixed it.'

'Wow.' Seb sat back and ran his hands through his hair. The muscles in his arms and chest flexed and Luci averted her gaze so she wasn't tempted to throw herself into his arms. 'Does Ben know?'

She shook her head. 'No.'

'Are you going to tell him?'

'I hadn't thought about it. Probably not. It doesn't matter to him any more. He's moved on. I have too. My marriage is over but now I have a chance to fulfil my dream of having a family. I *am* going to chase that dream. Which means I need to find the man who wants to follow that same dream, the man who wants to share my future. I know that's not what you want so I need to say goodbye.'

'Now?'

Luci nodded. She knew it would be hard. It was so tempting to spend their last remaining nights together but she knew the longer she waited the harder it would get. If her heart was going to break she wanted to get it over and done with.

'You'll be gone in a few days anyway. We both knew it was only a bit of fun, just a temporary arrangement. It was always a matter of when, not if, and I need to move on to the next phase of my life. I appreciate every minute, everything we have shared, you have helped me more than you'll ever know. I know I'm ready to let some-one else into my life now.'

'What are you going to do?'

'I'm not sure yet. Finish off my last two weeks here while I try to work out what this all means and then I don't know what. But I'm not going back to Vickers Hill. I doubt the man for me is there and I'm not sure that a big city is for me either.'

'So that's it? This is goodbye?'

She nodded, forcing herself to stay strong. 'We don't want the same things, Seb. We've both been honest about that. I was always going to want to find a way to have a family. You've always said that isn't on your agenda. I need to go.'

Now was his chance to tell her he'd changed his mind. That he couldn't live without her. She held her breath, waiting to see what he would do.

'Okay.' Seb sat forward, resting his elbows on his knees, and sighed. Luci stretched out one hand, wanting to run it over his back, but she hesitated just inches from his skin then pulled her hand away. She didn't know if he wanted or needed comfort.

Seb pushed himself to his feet and turned to face her. His blue eyes were still troubled but his voice was strong. He nodded his head. 'I respect the fact it's your decision to make. I'll just grab a few things and I'll sleep on the boat.'

Disappointment flooded Luci's chest and surged through her belly. She'd pinned her hopes on him changing his mind, even though she'd known it was a long shot, and it was devastating to know that he wasn't going to argue with her. That he wasn't going to change his mind. But neither was she.

She wanted to tell him that he didn't need to leave tonight but then realised it was probably better if he did. He wasn't the man for her future. He had been a perfect interlude but she couldn't let emotion derail her dreams.

But saying goodbye to Seb took some of the gloss off her dream. Gaining the knowledge that she could have kids meant she was losing him.

She needed to remember he had never really been hers in the first place.

This was goodbye.

She loved him but that was irrelevant. She had said she would give her right arm to have a chance at motherhood; giving up Seb was much harder.

She wasn't going to let the chance to have a baby feel like a consolation prize. She wanted a child more than anything. She had to remember that. But that didn't stop the tears from flowing again as she watched him walk out the door with his duffel bag and bike helmet. He travelled light, leaving only with what he'd come with, and taking her heart with him.

CHAPTER TEN

SEB HAD FINISHED his stint at the family and community health clinic. He was gone and Luci was doing her best to focus on her job. She had two days left before she went back to Vickers Hill for Christmas. She still hadn't decided what she would do after that. She'd make a final decision after the Christmas break. Hopefully by then her head would have cleared and she'd be able to think straight. She was having difficulty focusing, her thoughts turning constantly to Seb, and her heart was hurting so badly it was making her feel nauseous. She knew she had done the right thing, saying goodbye to him, but that wasn't making it any less painful.

The nausea was so bad today that she'd actually vomited up her breakfast and hadn't been able to keep anything down since. She felt like she might have contracted a virus. She had five minutes before her next appointment so she quickly took her temperature while she checked her emails. There was one from the doctor's wife in Budgee and Luci noticed it had been copied to Seb. She scanned the message. The doctor's wife had forwarded it from Nadine. She had wanted to send photos of her twins to Seb and Luci.

Luci opened the attachment. The twins appeared to be thriving. It was amazing to see how much they had developed in four weeks. They were both starting to fill out and their chocolate-brown eyes were shining. Luci felt a pang of envy but she had hope now and the knowledge that one day she might be holding a baby of her own in her arms was making it easier to cope with all the pregnant clients and newborn babies she seemed to have on her list.

After an uncertain start in community health she was now enjoying getting to know her patients and being able to give continuity of care was rewarding. It was very different from working in a hospital and she had managed to establish good relationships with several of the regular clients, which was extremely satisfying. Melanie Parsons was a good example. She and her kids had been in to see her several times and Melanie appeared to be coping much better. She and her husband were both attending counselling and her husband had also joined AA. Luci was pleased that she had been able to witness what she hoped would be the start of something better for their family. Seeing the change in Melanie and getting emails from patients like Nadine made her feel that she was making a difference and doing something worthwhile, even if her heart was breaking.

The thermometer beeped and Luci closed her emails and read the display as her diary flashed to indicate that her next client had arrived. Her temperature was slightly elevated—she'd take something for that after she'd finished her next consult.

'What can I help you with today, Shauna?' she asked as her client sat and settled her toddler on her knee.

'I think I might be pregnant again.'

Luci waited for the usual stab of jealousy but it didn't come. She didn't need to feel jealous any more, she was certain pregnancy would happen for her one day. 'Have you done a test?'

'I've done a couple,' Shauna said. 'One came back positive and one was negative but I've got all the usual symptoms. I feel sick, my boobs hurt and I need to go to the toilet constantly. I thought maybe you could do another test.'

Luci took a jar for a urine sample from the cupboard and handed it to Shauna.

She tested it when Shauna returned. 'It's negative. When was your last period?'

'Three weeks ago.'

'It might just be too early.'

The conversation made Luci think of her own situation. When had her last period been? she wondered. She did a quick mental calculation. It had been almost six weeks ago.

She and Seb had practised safe sex most of the time but that night on Seb's boat, during the thunderstorm and in the heat of the moment, protection had been the last thing on her mind. She hadn't thought anything of it then. Sex that night had been spontaneous, contraception hadn't been an issue for her then, and she hadn't given it a moment's thought.

Maybe she was pregnant?

But that eventuality was more than likely just wishful thinking. Mind over matter. She was probably putting two and two together and getting five, she thought. But the minute Shauna left the consulting room she took a standard pregnancy test from the cupboard for herself.

She took it into the bathroom. She knew what she was looking for. She'd done dozens of these. She was looking for two pink lines.

She waited. She'd never seen the two pink lines before.

Until today.

She double-checked the window. She leaned over the basin and triple-checked but the lines still remained.

Her knees buckled and she sat back on the toilet seat.

That explained the nausea and her slightly elevated temperature.

Her hand went to her stomach.

She was pregnant.

Seb was into his second week of holidays. He should be somewhere far away from Sydney. His plan had been to take his boat and travel but he hadn't been able to bring himself to leave. Not while Luci was still in town.

He'd realised too late that he should never have left so hurriedly the night Luci had said goodbye. He should have stayed and argued his case, only he hadn't known he'd had a case. Not then.

His knee-jerk reaction had been to leave. He didn't want to settle down, to commit—at least, that was what he'd been telling himself for three years—and it had taken him a while to realise he'd changed his mind. That *Luci* had made him change his mind. She had brought the light back into his life and her absence had taken it away again.

They had said goodbye but he hadn't been able

to sever the ties so he sat on his boat, alone, in Fairlight Bay, watching the lights go on and off in Callum's apartment and wondering what Luci was up to. How she was doing. If she was missing him.

For the past three years he had been working toward fixing his boat, making it habitable on a permanent basis, but now he felt trapped. It was supposed to be his sanctuary but instead it felt like a prison cell. He escaped its confines every day, taking his bike from the garage he'd rented and cruising the highways, but the feeling of freedom never lasted. He didn't want to be free. He didn't want to be able to come and go as he pleased. He didn't want to be alone. He wanted to be with Luci.

He shouldn't miss her and he knew he should be pleased for her. She had an opportunity to be a mother, had a chance to get what she'd always wanted. But he wanted that to be him.

He had spent the last three years convincing himself, and everyone else, that he was fine, that he was happy to be alone, but he hadn't stopped to see if he actually was and now that Luci was gone from his life and he was alone again he realised that he wasn't okay. He needed her in his life.

He needed her.

He loved her.

And he didn't want to think about Luci finding another man. He didn't want to give someone else the chance he'd thrown away.

Once again he hadn't realised how badly he wanted something until it was gone but, unlike last time, it wasn't too late. He wanted Luci in his life and he would do what he could to keep her.

She wanted a family and he wanted her. Could he give her what she wanted?

He was going to have to because he couldn't imagine his life without her in it.

All he needed to know was whether or not she wanted him.

He knew she was due to leave Sydney tomorrow but he didn't know where she was headed. What were her plans? What was she going to do?

He only had a few hours to find out. It was two

days until Christmas and Luci was due to leave Sydney on Christmas Eve.

He had one last chance to see her.

Luci had finished cleaning the apartment. She was leaving tomorrow. She would be back in Vickers Hill for Christmas.

She went into Callum's bedroom, just for one final check to make sure it was clean and tidy, although she knew it was. Seb had changed the sheets and tidied up. She knew because she was in here every day, thinking about him. She sat on the bed and ran her hands over the covers. They were tucked tight, not a stray crease in sight. Almost as if Seb had never been there.

She thought about the first night they'd made love. It had been in this bed. They'd been in too much of a hurry to get any further; they'd barely made it to here. But the bed showed no sign of their intimacy. It was almost as if it never happened.

But she had proof that it wasn't a dream.

Her hand went to her stomach.

There was the proof of what they had shared. She had all the proof she needed.

She had two things left to do—pack her bags and then see if she could get hold of Seb.

She had debated about when she should speak to him, when she should give him the news. She had thought about waiting until thirteen weeks, or maybe even eighteen, after her first scan, until she knew everything was all right, but she had decided it would be better to tell him face-to-face while she was still in Sydney, and she knew part of her wanted an excuse to see him one last time before she left.

There would be no easy way to share her news and she knew he didn't like surprises but he had the right to know about the baby. Their baby.

He had the right to have the opportunity to choose to be involved. Or not. She had no idea what he would choose to do but that was his prerogative.

Luci hadn't really ever expected to end up a single mother. Before the phone call from her GP she had assumed she would have to adopt in order to have a family and adopting in South Australia meant she needed a partner. She had assumed she would need to find a man.

But now she had the opportunity she'd been wanting—the chance to be a mother. A month ago she would have leapt at the chance, any chance, to hold a baby of her own in her arms, so why did she now want more? She knew she could manage on her own. She knew she didn't need a partner. The trouble was, this wasn't about what she needed. It was about what she wanted.

So she was getting what she'd always wanted, except now she wanted more. She wanted Seb too.

Although she knew she should be content with what was in store for her, it was hard when her heart ached constantly for what was missing from her life. She had traded one heartache for another. Why couldn't she have it all?

She stood up. She needed to get moving. Procrastination never solved anything.

She was staring at the clothes in her wardrobe,

wondering where to start, when she was inter-rupted by a knock on the door.

She opened the door and burst into tears.

Seb was standing on the other side.

'Luci, what on earth's the matter?' he asked as he stepped across the threshold. He opened his arms and gathered her up, holding her close.

She let him comfort her. She was right where she wanted to be. If only she could just stay here, maybe everything would turn out as she hoped.

She cried into his shoulder and sniffed as she said, 'Nothing, I'm just tired. I haven't been sleeping well.' *Plus I'm an emotional wreck and I'm carrying your baby.* But that was *not* the way to deliver her news.

'Are you unwell?'

He stepped back, releasing her from his arms but not letting go completely. It felt good to have her in his arms again but he'd needed to see her. He'd needed to make sure she was okay. She looked like she had lost weight and her blue-grey eyes were filled with tears, but otherwise she looked fantastic. Her skin glowed and she looked perfectly healthy.

'No,' she said. 'I'm fine. I'm glad you're here.'

'Are you sure? You don't look happy to see me.'

She laughed and Seb breathed a sigh of relief. She sounded like the Luci he loved, full of laughter and happiness even if she had just been sobbing in his arms.

'Of course I am. I've missed you.'

Good. That cheered him up. Perhaps things would turn out in his favour. 'I've missed you too.'

She was looking up at him. Her eyes were shining and her pink lips were slightly parted, like an opening rosebud. He had come here to talk to her, to beg her for another chance, but he couldn't resist. He bent his head and kissed her.

She sighed gently and leaned into him and he felt her arms loop around his neck as she kissed him back. Soft and supple in his arms, he could feel his soul being restored as he held her. She tasted like heaven and he wished he could stay like this for eternity.

But he needed to find out if that was possible.

'Luci,' he sighed as he pulled away. He kept a finger under her chin, keeping her face tilted up at him. 'I need to talk to you.'

'Oh.' Something flashed behind her eyes. Was it disappointment?

He took her hand and led her to the couch. The place was spotless and its tidiness served to remind him that his time was limited. If he didn't get this problem resolved tonight, it would be too late. She would be gone.

He kept hold of her hand as they sat, making her sit close to him.

'What is it?' she asked. 'Is something wrong?'

Seb nodded. 'Yes. I've made a mistake. A big one. But I'm hoping it's not too late to fix it. I've discovered a pattern.'

'A pattern?'

'It's a problem I have,' he told her, 'where I can't seem to work out I want something until it's gone. But I'm hoping this time I haven't left it too late.'

'I'm not following you. Left what too late?'

'Us. I don't want to lose you. I don't want to let you go.' He picked up her other hand, holding them both, keeping her close. 'You have brought light back into my life. A purpose. An energy. A reason to look forward to the day. I didn't know what my life was lacking until you came into it. I thought I was okay on my own. Happy even. But I was kidding myself. I was surviving. I wasn't living and I definitely wasn't happy.

'I've missed you,' he said honestly. 'I look for you, I listen for you. I want to hear your laugh, I want to see your smile. I want to be the one who *makes* you smile. I don't want you to leave. I came here tonight to ask if you would consider staying in Sydney. With me. I want to see if we can make something of this thing between us. Before it's too late.'

He very rarely spoke about his feelings and he certainly hadn't bared as much of his soul in the past three years but it didn't seem to make any difference. Luci was shaking her head. 'It *is* too late. I'm going home.'

'Back to Vickers Hill?'

She nodded.

Seb's heart plummeted like a stone and settled heavily and morosely in his abdomen. He was losing her. 'I thought you'd decided that wasn't the place for you.'

'My circumstances have changed.'

How much could have changed in two weeks? Did she feel nothing for him?

'Have you met someone else?' Surely she couldn't have moved on that quickly? He didn't want to think of her with other men. He didn't want to imagine her searching for someone else to share her dream. What was wrong with him? Why couldn't she choose him?

'No, of course not. This is a practical decision. A financial one. I can't afford to start again.'

Despite the flicker of hope that had come to life as soon as Seb had started talking, Luci had other things to consider now. Another *person* to consider. She couldn't allow herself to get carried away until she was sure of Seb's feelings. Vickers Hill had been good enough for her growing up, it was a good place to raise a family and she would have support there. All the things she had hated at times about a small country town were now the reasons she was moving back. She knew people would rally around her. If she was going to be a single mother she wanted to do it somewhere familiar. Somewhere safe. 'This is the next stage of my journey.'

'Can you take that next stage with me?'

She shook her head, still determined not to jump head first too soon. 'You know I can't. You know what I want. Being a mother is something I've always wanted. If I have to choose between having a family and having you, I will choose children. I'm sorry. I wish I could have both but that's up to you.'

Luci had dreamed of Seb choosing to be with her but he had to choose everything. He had to choose her dream as well as her. This was her chance to see how he felt without telling him about the baby. She didn't want to force his hand, she didn't want him to feel that he had to make promises he wouldn't be able to keep, but she had nothing to lose now. If he didn't want a family she could still walk away.

'Luci, I love you and I want a future with you.'

'You love me?'

'I do. I know you want a family and I'm asking you to give me a chance. Let's see if we can have that future together.'

'I can't afford to wait. I haven't got time to see if it all works out. I can't.' She took a deep breath. It was now or never. She was either going to get what she wished for or not but either way the time had come to share her news. 'I'm already pregnant.'

'What? When? How?'

'The usual way, I suppose. Ironic, isn't it? I didn't think it could happen for me the usual way but it must have been that night on the boat.'

'In the storm?'

Luci nodded. 'I'm sorry. I know you hate surprises but you need to know.'

'Don't be sorry.' Seb shook his head and his eyes filled with tears. 'I'm going to be a father?'

Luci nodded. She took his hand and put it on

her stomach as her nerves escalated another notch. Her dream was so close she could almost taste it and she couldn't stand the thought that it might all slip away. She tried one last time to convince him that things could work out. 'I know loving someone scares you and I understand that this is a big step for you, but you have to have faith that things will be okay. Bad things can happen but they don't always happen. You can't close yourself off just in case you get hurt. I intend to live my life and I want you to live yours. But I would like us to live our lives together, I'd like us to share our dreams. I love you and I think we can make this work but it's up to you. I know this will be a shock, it's a lot to take in and I don't expect you to decide what you want to do tonight, but you should know that I am going to have the baby.'

'Of course you are. And I'm going to be there with you. Every step of the way.'

'Are you sure?'

'Positive. I'm ready for this. I know you didn't want to fall for the first guy who crossed your

path and I wanted to give you a chance to decide
if you wanted me. That was why I thought we
could take our time and see what happened but
I know I want you. I know I want a future with
you. And a family. I have thought about nothing
else for the past two weeks.'

Seb reached for her. Brushing her hair from her
face, he bent his head and kissed her and Luci
could feel herself blossoming under his touch.

'I love you, Luci, and I promise that will never
change.' He smiled at her and his blue eyes sparkled as he added, 'And now you need to invite
me home with you for Christmas.'

'You want to come with me?'

'Where else would I be? I want to spend the
rest of my life with you and that starts now. Plus
I think it's time I met your parents. I need to ask
your father for your hand in marriage.'

'You want to get married?'

'I do.'

'My father won't expect you to ask his permis-
sion.'

'I think he will and I'd like to do things properly. I need to at least tell him I intend to make an honest woman out of his only daughter before I tell him I knocked her up.'

Luci laughed. 'They probably wouldn't believe you. It's incredible, isn't it?'

Seb nodded. 'It's amazing.' He got off the couch and went down on one knee. He slid his hands under the hem of her shirt, exposing her belly. He kissed it gently and the touch of his lips sent flames of desire racing through her. His hands were on her knees and she felt her thighs fall apart under the caress of his fingers as she waited for him to slide his hands up her legs, but his fingers went no further. He knelt between her thighs but his focus was on her face.

'I came here to see if I could convince you to give me a chance to prove my love. I want to share your dreams with you. I want to share your life. Will you let me love you and our children for the rest of our lives? Will you marry me? Will you be my wife?'

Luci pulled Seb to his feet and wrapped herself in his arms. She kissed him deeply, fighting back tears. Her dreams were coming true but it was not the time for tears. She was getting everything she'd wanted since the moment she'd first laid eyes on Seb. This glorious, gorgeous man wanted to make a life with her and she wasn't going to refuse him.

'I will.'

EPILOGUE

LUCI SAT ON the front veranda and watched the sun rise over the ocean as she nursed her baby. This was one of her favourite times of day.

She and Seb had the best of both worlds. They had moved to the coastal town of Shellharbour after their wedding but were still only a two-hour drive from Manly. They could have a day in the city if they wanted and return to the relative peace and quiet of a large country town. They both had jobs at the local hospital in family and community health, and Luci was considering studying midwifery, but she had time to make that decision. Their daughter, Eve, was only four months old, she still had a couple of months of maternity leave and would only be going back to work part time. They had jobs they enjoyed, a lifestyle they loved, but most importantly they had their family.

Sometimes Luci could hardly breathe when she thought about how wonderful her life was and how much it had changed. Blessed with a daughter, a gorgeous husband and a new life in Shellharbour, she still sometimes wanted to pinch herself.

She lifted her daughter from her breast and held her up against her shoulder, inhaling her scent of talcum powder, baby lotion and love.

She looked up as she heard soft footsteps on the wooden floorboards. Their house was full of visitors but she'd recognise that rhythm anywhere.

Seb stepped out onto the balcony, followed by the two-year-old Labrador they had somehow inherited with their house. She smiled as she thought about the man she had first met—the motorcycle-riding man who'd been adamant that he was going to live a bachelor life on his boat. Now he was a husband, a father, a home owner and a pet owner who had swapped regular trips to the country with a permanent job in a country town. He had traded his motorbike for a family car but he still had his boat, which he'd named *Diamond Sky*, which was moored in the marina five minutes from home. Their lives had changed dramatically in the course of a year but she knew he was happy and content.

'Merry Christmas, my love.'

Luci lifted her face for a kiss as Seb put a mug of green tea beside her and plucked Eve from her arms.

'Come here, my gorgeous girl.'

Eve gurgled and laughed and reached for her father with chubby little hands. She was a real daddy's girl but Luci didn't mind. She was living her dream.

'You're up early,' Seb said.

He was bare-chested and Luci felt the familiar stirring of longing as she looked at him. Even the sleepless nights associated with a new baby hadn't been able to diminish her desire for her husband.

'You know I love it out here and I didn't want to wake everyone else.'

Seb's parents were staying with them for Christmas. Seb's dad in particular was smitten with Eve and Luci knew that her in-laws saw this time as an opportunity to enjoy the things they'd missed out on with their own boys. Luci's own parents, not wanting to be separated from their first grandchild, had decided to retire to Shellharbour and lived just down the road, and Callum and Flick were also under their roof. Eve was being christened tomorrow and Cal and Flick were to be her godparents.

'We haven't taken on too much, have we? Hosting Christmas and then having Eve's christening?' Seb asked.

Luci shook her head. She was surrounded by family and she couldn't be happier. 'No. This is just what I wanted. Having everyone here with us is perfect.' She stood up and wrapped her arms around Seb and their daughter. 'Life is perfect,' she said as she raised herself onto her toes and kissed her husband. 'I love you. I love you both.'

* * * * *

Look out for the next great story in
THE CHRISTMAS SWAP *duet*

*SWEPT AWAY BY THE SEDUCTIVE
STRANGER
by Amy Andrews*

*And if you enjoyed this story, check out these
other great reads from Emily Forbes:*

*FALLING FOR THE SINGLE DAD
A LOVE AGAINST ALL ODDS
HIS LITTLE CHRISTMAS MIRACLE
A KISS TO MELT HER HEART*

All available now!

MILLS & BOON®
Large Print Medical

May

The Nurse's Christmas Gift	Tina Beckett
The Midwife's Pregnancy Miracle	Kate Hardy
Their First Family Christmas	Alison Roberts
The Nightshift Before Christmas	Annie O'Neil
It Started at Christmas...	Janice Lynn
Unwrapped by the Duke	Amy Ruttan

June

White Christmas for the Single Mum	Susanne Hampton
A Royal Baby for Christmas	Scarlet Wilson
Playboy on Her Christmas List	Carol Marinelli
The Army Doc's Baby Bombshell	Sue MacKay
The Doctor's Sleigh Bell Proposal	Susan Carlisle
Christmas with the Single Dad	Louisa Heaton

July

Falling for Her Wounded Hero	Marion Lennox
The Surgeon's Baby Surprise	Charlotte Hawkes
Santiago's Convenient Fiancée	Annie O'Neil
Alejandro's Sexy Secret	Amy Ruttan
The Doctor's Diamond Proposal	Annie Claydon
Weekend with the Best Man	Leah Martyn

MILLS & BOON®
Large Print Medical

August

Their Meant-to-Be Baby	Caroline Anderson
A Mummy for His Baby	Molly Evans
Rafael's One Night Bombshell	Tina Beckett
Dante's Shock Proposal	Amalie Berlin
A Forever Family for the Army Doc	Meredith Webber
The Nurse and the Single Dad	Dianne Drake

September

Their Secret Royal Baby	Carol Marinelli
Her Hot Highland Doc	Annie O'Neil
His Pregnant Royal Bride	Amy Ruttan
Baby Surprise for the Doctor Prince	Robin Gianna
Resisting Her Army Doc Rival	Sue MacKay
A Month to Marry the Midwife	Fiona McArthur

October

Their One Night Baby	Carol Marinelli
Forbidden to the Playboy Surgeon	Fiona Lowe
A Mother to Make a Family	Emily Forbes
The Nurse's Baby Secret	Janice Lynn
The Boss Who Stole Her Heart	Jennifer Taylor
Reunited by Their Pregnancy Surprise	Louisa Heaton

MILLS & BOON®
Large Print – May 2017

ROMANCE

A Deal for the Di Sione Ring	Jennifer Hayward
The Italian's Pregnant Virgin	Maisey Yates
A Dangerous Taste of Passion	Anne Mather
Bought to Carry His Heir	Jane Porter
Married for the Greek's Convenience	Michelle Smart
Bound by His Desert Diamond	Andie Brock
A Child Claimed by Gold	Rachael Thomas
Her New Year Baby Secret	Jessica Gilmore
Slow Dance with the Best Man	Sophie Pembroke
The Prince's Convenient Proposal	Barbara Hannay
The Tycoon's Reluctant Cinderella	Therese Beharrie

HISTORICAL

The Wedding Game	Christine Merrill
Secrets of the Marriage Bed	Ann Lethbridge
Compromising the Duke's Daughter	Mary Brendan
In Bed with the Viking Warrior	Harper St. George
Married to Her Enemy	Jenni Fletcher

MEDICAL

The Nurse's Christmas Gift	Tina Beckett
The Midwife's Pregnancy Miracle	Kate Hardy
Their First Family Christmas	Alison Roberts
The Nightshift Before Christmas	Annie O'Neil
It Started at Christmas...	Janice Lynn
Unwrapped by the Duke	Amy Ruttan

0417 GEN STD LP

7